THE RUSSIAN LIEUTENANT

Peter Marshall

London | New York

Published by Clink Street Publishing 2020

Copyright © 2020

First edition.

The author asserts the moral right under the Copyright, Designs and Patents Act 1988 to be identified as the author of this work.

All rights reserved. No part of this publication may be reproduced, stored in a retrieval system or transmitted, in any form or by any means without the prior consent of the author, nor be otherwise circulated in any form of binding or cover other than that with which it is published and without a similar condition being imposed on the subsequent purchaser.

*ISBN:
978-1-913340-72-8 paperback
978-1-913340-73-5 ebook*

Contents

AUTHOR'S FOREWORD   v

1.	EXPECTATION	1
2.	NIKOLAI'S PLAN	8
3.	MARINA'S MOVE TO PORTSMOUTH	17
4.	"DOROGAYA"	24
5.	INTERROGATION	33
6.	THE TIP-OFF!	38
7.	"A RUSSIAN SPY?"	46
8.	OFFICIAL SECRETS ACT	50
9.	THE LAWYER	60
10.	"FIND MARINA"	70
11.	RUSSIAN CONSULAR VISIT	72
12.	IGOR AND SVETLANA	78
13.	THE FARMHOUSE	83
14.	VICTOR PETERS ARRIVES	88
15.	A MAN NAMED JACK	93
16.	THE "SAFE" FLAT	97
17.	ALDANOV IN COURT	100
18.	AN MI5 RECRUIT?	104
19.	INTRODUCING "MARY"	110
20.	MEANWHILE IN PUTNEY	113
21.	IT'S DISNEYWORLD	120
22.	A BOMBSHELL!	127
23.	LEARNING RUSSIAN	130
24.	"MARY" RETURNS	135

25.	NO SPYING TRIAL	140
26.	THE SPY SWAP	144
27.	BACK HOME	148
28.	THE CRIME SCENE	152
29.	WHO POISONED MARINA?	158
30.	A RED ROSE	165

AUTHOR'S FOREWORD

During my varied career, I served as an officer in the Royal Navy and in the reserves with the RNVR; I lived for a few years in historic Old Portsmouth, with a view across the Solent; I became a journalist for local and national newspapers and then the BBC; and later I worked in the satellite communications business in United States for 12 years before turning to writing in my retirement (and having eight books published).

Readers will probably recognise these experiences as providing a framework for my story about Marina and the unexpected consequences of her on-line date with the Russian Lieutenant, introducing her into the ruthless world of international espionage.

All the individuals named in this story are fictitious, and if they bear any resemblance to real people, alive or deceased, this is entirely coincidental. Most of the locations and events described in the book are also fictitious – with a few exceptions which I think readers will find self-explanatory.

Peter Marshall
Dorset, UK
2020

1.
EXPECTATION

Like thousands of others over the years, Marina was waiting on the sea wall by the old Semaphore Tower at the entrance to Portsmouth harbour, peering anxiously out to sea. Through the October morning mist, she was looking for that first glimpse of an approaching ship, just as wives and girlfriends had done since the years of sailing ships, always hopeful they were bringing their menfolk safely home.

But unlike all the others before her, Marina was waiting to welcome a man she had never met.

After spending her childhood, schooldays and early working career in South London, Marina Peters now felt at home in Portsmouth, a vibrant and expanding city combining a long seafaring history with modern developments. As she waited, she reflected on how much she had enjoyed the first three years of her new life there and being by the sea. There were all the attractions of the resort area of Southsea – with its seafront and beaches and the ferries chugging their way to the Isle of Wight and Gosport – and the enticing sight of large cruise liners passing through the Solent to and from Southampton. And of course, there was the glamour of the Royal Navy, its ships and its sailors, and the always impressive Royal Marines.

She had made new friends in her office in the Portsmouth

Dockyard, went to occasional parties and had started a couple of new relationships with interesting men she met – which had both fizzled out too soon. She signed up to join a local choir group, doing occasional concerts and widening her circle of friends. She enjoyed evenings at the cinema and tried not to become too dependent on the temptations of computer games and online shopping … until one life-changing evening.

Encouraged and intrigued by the experiences she heard about from others in her office, and from stories she read in magazines and newspapers, she decided to explore social media and dating websites.

Soon, she was hooked. Two or three times a week, at home in her small Southsea flat, she sat at her laptop computer late into the evening scanning the "find a friend" sites. In reality, she found very few pictures and descriptions which deserved more than a passing glance … until her attention focussed, one night, on Nikolai Aldanov. He was a handsome 35-year-old Russian, wearing a smart uniform, who said he was a widower with no children. He said he spoke good English and had special interests in literature and history and wanted to meet a lady who would help him to know more about these subjects, particularly from a British angle. But it was Marina's own Russian ancestry which made her read this entry more than once.

Her grandparents, Vlad and Marina Petrov, were Russian immigrants to Britain in the 1930s. Through friends, they had both found work in the warehouse of a London company in the docklands importing fabrics from Eastern Europe and the Far East. They were ambitious and, after working hard for a couple of years, they had learned enough about the business to rent a small shop, with a flat above, in a South London suburb. And there, with their savings, they started a small shop retailing those imported fabrics.

It became a struggle in the years after the outbreak of war in September 1939, but they were accustomed to difficult times and kept going. They had two sons, Viktor and Anatoly, who were born during the early days of the war, and like so many East London families, they prayed and kept going and their home and business were fortunate to survive the wartime bombing unscathed.

In 1945, they were proud survivors and decided to become British citizens, Anglicising their name to Peters. It was Marina's father, now Victor Peters, and her uncle, now called Andrew, who eventually followed in their parents' footsteps and started work in the shop when they left school at 16. The fabrics business had flourished and expanded in the post-war rebuilding of London, and in the 1960s, Vlad retired, and his ambitious sons took over and continued to grow the business successfully.

The Peters family also grew. Victor married Shona, who had become one of his best customers. She was an Irish-born interior designer working in London's West End, and they settled into a new and comfortable home in the Thamesside suburb of Putney. It was there, in the late 1980s, that all the family gathered to celebrate the arrival of Marina, the new baby who was given her grandmother's name.

As she grew up, and especially at family gatherings, Marina was fascinated by the stories they told, particularly those about her ancestors' struggles in the impoverished city of Voronezh in Southwest Russia and how her grandfather, Vlad Petrov, and his wife had decided to seek a new life in Britain. They were ambitious and bold and had heard stories from others in the town about the new opportunities to be found by travelling westwards.

And so, with few possessions and little money, the two of them had journeyed in stages across Europe by trains and buses and, finally, the cross-channel ferry to Dover. From there, tired and almost penniless, they had travelled by bus to seek out their only contact, "the friend of a friend" who lived in south London's Russian community. These family conversations often went on to recall the story of how much of the home city they had left behind in 1935, had become a battle-scarred ruin in the Second World War; and how many of their friends and relations back there had perished or were driven out to become homeless in the surrounding areas; and how Voronezh, ignored for many years, had now been rebuilt into a thriving, modern metropolis. As she grew into her teens, Marina's ambition to visit her roots grew stronger and stronger.

It was with these family memories flowing through her mind that Nikolai's picture began to glow more vividly on her computer screen. Marina began to put together her first response, then paused for second thoughts, then deleted it. She looked at the information on her screen carefully, again and again; should she ignore her cautious instincts – just this once?

But there was nothing to lose, she decided, and she could always say "no". So, gathering her resolve, she started again – and finally made a positive contact.

She had already signed into the website with her name and age, so she just needed to tick the box alongside the entry with its photograph of Nikolai Aldanov… and wait.

After a couple of minutes, the screen came to life.

"Hello Marina," came the first response. *"Where are you?"*

"In England – I live in the city of Portsmouth. Where are you?"

"Hello. I was not expecting to hear from England, so this is very exciting for me. I am in the Russian navy port of Sevastopol in the Crimea. And I think Portsmouth is a naval port too?"

"Yes, it is – that is an interesting coincidence. I think I recognised your Navy uniform in your photograph. I see lots of naval officers here."

"I am sure you do. Can you send me a photograph, too, Marina? That's a nice name, and it will be even nicer to see who I am chatting to?"

"Yes, of course." And Marina quickly opened one of her favourites from her photo file and used the online system to copy it into their exchange of messages. It showed her with a glass of champagne at a recent birthday party, looking her glamorous best.

"That's very nice," replied Nikolai. *"Where was that taken?"*

"It was my best friend's 30th birthday party last month in London, where I used to live … but I only drink champagne on very special occasions."

"Well, this is a special occasion. Let's drink to our meeting up like this. I would like to know more about you, but I have to go now. When can we try to get together again?"

They agreed to connect on-line again on the following Sunday evening at about 6 pm for Marina and 9 pm for Nikolai. She was slightly surprised, but pleased, to find that he was there and waiting when Marina signed on again as arranged, and they began to exchange more information. He told her he was a Lieutenant in the Navy, and she, in turn, described how she had moved from London three years ago to start a new career working for the British navy as a civilian in an office job, based in the Portsmouth Dockyard.

"Well we do have some interests in common," Nikolai typed. Marina warmed to the topic and told him that there was yet another common interest because her grandfather had come from Russia in the 1930s to start a new life in London. And she admitted that it was partly this Russian ancestry which had drawn her to respond to Nikolai's on-line listing.

After a few weeks of chatting once or twice a week about their respective lives, he became intrigued as Marina told him more about her grandparents' memories of Russia. She told him how they had lived in poverty before deciding to try to find a new life in Britain, following in the footsteps of others from their neighbourhood, and how they had eventually started their own business in London. She said she longed to pay a visit someday to Voronezh, the city where they had lived, to explore what she could of their background. He told her that Voronezh was not too far from Sevastopol and he offered to help her to discover her roots, if and when she could find an opportunity to travel to Russia.

Nikolai was also interested to discover more about Portsmouth and Marina's work in the Dockyard, and she explained that it was with the Royal Navy in the offices of the Commodore of the Portsmouth-based fleet.

"It's fairly low-level stuff," she wrote in reply to his question, *"But it's very interesting because we deal with all the communications between the HQ and the ships at sea."*

"Sounds a bit like my present job," he responded. *"But I really preferred being on a ship to having an office job."*

Their correspondence became more and more personal over the weeks, and they exchanged photographs from their younger days, of their homes and families and their travels. He said his wife had died tragically in childbirth five years earlier, and he was now alone instead of being the family man he had hoped for; he had faced the challenge of building a new life around his career in the Navy. His parents were now in retirement, living not far from Sevastopol, and he had a very supportive older sister, Anna, who helped to care for them.

The plan for Marina to visit Russia began to evolve, perhaps during a period in the next year during Nikolai's annual leave, when he would have time to be her "tour guide", and she said how much she looked forward to meeting his friends and family. And they each spoke warmly about getting to know each other better.

She started to research flights and fares from London to Russia. And with gathering excitement, she also began to assemble a file on the history of Voronezh and the local region – until one evening when Nikolai came on-line with a surprise.

"I have some big news," he wrote. *"My wish has been granted. I have been appointed to join a ship again – it is a really modern frigate called the Admiral Essen, based here in Sevastopol. It is really exciting because it is one of a group of three ships from the Black Sea fleet which will go on exercises during the next month in the Mediterranean. And can you believe this – we are then scheduled to sail on to the Atlantic Ocean and will be making courtesy visits to several foreign ports – including a few days in Portsmouth!"*

This was sudden and unexpected news for Marina.

"This is wonderful!" she said in her reply. *"I hope this means we will be able to meet up sooner than we expected and maybe spend some time together. Let me know more details and dates as soon as you can so that I can arrange some time off work."*

Once she had fully absorbed this new situation, she began to focus, instead of travel plans, on ways to welcome him to her own country and their first meeting when it came, presumably in the coming autumn months. There would be no more chat on the dating website, and it was a couple of weeks before Nikolai's next message, an e-mail, in which he told Marina that he was now on board his ship and settling in as they prepared to sail. He explained that once his ship had sailed and was involved in exercises at sea, their contacts would become less frequent.

Marina waited patiently for more news. And in the course of her job in the Dockyard communications office, she soon learned more information about plans for a forthcoming visit by ships from the Russian navy for refuelling in Portsmouth.

And then, she received a brief message from Nikolai with a firm date for their arrival and confirming his intention to meet up with her "at the earliest opportunity".

2.
NIKOLAI'S PLAN

In the headquarters of Russia's GRU Secret Service in Grizodubovoy Street, Moscow, not far from the Kremlin, agent Aldanov asked for a meeting with his supervisor. Nikolai Aldanov was a well-regarded member of the research and analysis team. He was also an officer in the naval reserves after serving for seven years in the Russian Navy, mostly at sea on board warships. He had gained a commission and promotion to the rank of Lieutenant. But after completing his required seven years, during which he was married, he had been persuaded by his young wife to make a change. She was delighted when he applied for a job at the Ministry of Defence in Moscow, her home city. And after several interviews, he took his naval experience with him into a second career with the GRU.

The full name of the Russian ministry is the Directorate of the General Staff of the Armed Forces of the Russian Federation, commonly known by its previous name of the GRU. The labrynthine headquarters buildings house what was previously called the KGB until the break-up of the Soviet Union in 1991. But the organization, in which Vladimir Putin made his name, is still much the same, but is now called the FSB – the Federal Security Bureau.

It includes the GRU, the military intelligence agency of the Russian armed forces which, unlike other agencies, reports directly to the Minister of Defence. It is reputedly Russia's largest foreign intelligence agency and is the beating heart of Russia's spying operations.

After his training period, Aldanov was appointed to the research department of the agency, and one of his tasks, in the beehive of activity, was to analyse the myriad of websites and social media sites originating overseas. He and others in his team were searching for useful snippets of information which could be followed up by agents in the field. After a while, one of his own ideas was to insert his own photograph in naval uniform on several international dating websites, just to see what might follow.

When he was called up for the meeting he had requested with his "big boss", he said, "I think I may have found something interesting." He went on to describe how his dating efforts had eventually produced a response from a British woman working for the Royal Navy in Portsmouth. "And what is more, she had Russian grandparents," he added.

Asked what he had in mind, he explained, "I would like to have permission to open up a personal correspondence with this woman and try to discover by careful stages how useful she could be as a source. I would prefer not to involve our London office at this time, if you agree?"

The director gave him the go-ahead but asked to be kept closely informed.

Sadly, after just two years of their new life in Moscow, Aldanov's wife had died in childbirth, and he was given special leave to deal with his family matters. But he was soon anxious to get back to his duties, where he threw himself into his work and stayed late into the evenings to fill his time, refusing social invitations and even drinks with his colleagues. In particular, he believed that his unconventional "dating" idea would help to enhance his reputation in the department.

In between all his other investigative tasks, agent Aldanov began to develop the relationship with his British "date", and he was surprised by her willingness to respond so readily to his questions about her Russian background and her job. He took things deliberately slowly, and among all their friendly and sometimes more romantic exchanges, he was able to discover that she was single, about 30, with special interests in travel and an ambition to visit Russia. He was able to report to his director that she worked in the communications office of the British Navy's Portsmouth headquarters and had described how she was at the hub of information regarding fleet movements and the readiness of the ships of the fleet.

After a month or so of these on-line exchanges, he had worked out a plan to take his idea to the next stage. He asked for another meeting with his director and set out an operational proposal. "I think my contact in Britain is a real long-term prospect for us, if we handle it the right way," he said. "My suggestion is that we find the next ship which could realistically have a reason to call into a British port. I could then join the ship's company on some pretence and eventually arrange an opportunity to meet up with the woman to check her out face to face, as it were. I really think she is ready to meet me."

"I'll take further advice on this idea," came the cautious response. "Just keep the contact warm for the time being, and I will see what is in the future plans for the Navy that might work."

Nikolai Aldanov kept a low profile in the following days, but he became concerned when he received an inquiry from a senior intelligence officer based in the London embassy, asking for more information about his contact. He realised that his idea had leaked as a result of the further discussions between departments; because it involved the UK, someone had copied a memorandum about his plan to the London station of GRU. He stalled and decided not to reply to the London contact, insisting to his own director that if they decided to follow up in any way, the involvement by the agents there could put at risk the relationship he had been so carefully nurturing.

"If we are to get anywhere, I have to pursue this as a romantic attachment – or she will smell a rat," he said. "This woman could be pure gold if we play our cards right. Can you please call London off until I need their support?" He got a nod of agreement.

A couple of weeks passed before he was summoned to another meeting upstairs, where he found his director with a very senior naval commander in uniform, who began by asking, "Does your uniform still fit, or have you put on weight in this office job?"

He then went on to explain that an opportunity had occurred to test the plan and he surprised Aldanov by saying that it had been decided that he would join a frigate at Sevastapol in two days' time. This was the *Admiral Essen*, one of three ships due to sail in the next week for the Mediterranean on exercises. He would be appointed to the position of third Lieutenant in training, and neither the ship's captain or anyone else would be told the reason for his move from the reserve back into full operational duties. And he should certainly not reveal what his job had been in recent years; if he needed to say anything, he should say he had wanted a change following the loss of his wife.

Nikolai tried to suppress his delight and excitement at the prospect of not only returning to serve at sea, which he loved, but also the opportunity to follow up his own plan as part of his new career with the intelligence service. He had also come to rather like Marina! He returned to his office and began the task of clearing his desk. He handed over all his files to his surprised supervisor with the minimum of explanation about "a new job" and went home to pack. He also sent a brief e-mail message to Marina to say he was on his way. Next morning, he took the train from Moscow to Sevastapol.

In the naval dockyard area, he soon found the *Admiral Essen*, and once on board, he soon felt "back at home". He asked the sailor on gangway duty to take him to meet the First Officer, who gave him a warm welcome. They had been informed the previous day that a reserve officer would be joining them and he was shown to his designated cabin – small but comfortably equipped. There he met the steward who looked after the needs of the three Lieutenants on board – a luxury he had almost forgotten as the steward carefully unpacked and stowed his belongings. Close by were the slightly larger cabins of the Captain and First Officer and also two more cabins for the Electronics and Weapons Officer and the Chief Engineer. Between them, these officers led a crew of nearly 200, including some very experienced technical experts responsible for the latest armament and communications systems and for maintaining the ship's helicopter. During his first hours on board, he found opportunities to introduce himself to his fellow officers and was briefed on his sea-going duties by the Captain. The others had all served on this new frigate since it had been commissioned for service nearly a year earlier, but they were welcoming to the "new boy", and by the end of day one, he felt "ready to go" after nearly four years ashore in his new but secret career.

When they all gathered in the officers' dining room that evening, the others were understandably curious about his "desk job at the Defence Ministry", as he described it to them. But they seemed ready to accept his explanation that following the death of his wife, he had been able to pull a few strings and get back to active service again. His last sea-going job had been on a warship of an earlier generation, so he was particularly anxious to learn about all the more recent and sophisticated technical and electronic equipment he would find in his new ship, one of the latest class of frigates to join the Russian fleet.

Just three days later, the *Admiral Essen* sailed from Sebastapol into the Black Sea, together with the other two sister ships, and in the control centre behind the bridge, Nikolai studied the charts and their mission instructions, with guidance from one of his more experienced colleagues. He was ready to take over his first four-hour duty watch on the bridge that night.

From his more recent experience in Moscow, he knew that every movement of the ship and every message transmitted between the radio cabin and the naval base was being monitored – not only by his former colleagues in GRU but no doubt also by foreign agencies in Europe and the USA. There was no way that he could make contact with Marina now.

The ship's programme began with a series of practice manoeuvres and exercises during the 450-mile crossing of the Black Sea, which helped Nikolai and many of the ship's company to become familiar with the various capabilities of the *Admiral Essen*, until they had their first sight of the spectacular skyline of the Bosphorus on their third morning at sea. The traditional minarets and modern skyscrapers of Istanbul and the two suspension bridges glistened in the sunrise – tending to distract attention away from the task of navigating gently through the increasingly busy shipping as they passed through into the Sea of Marmora. For this tricky passage, as the second of the three frigates in convoy, the Captain was on the bridge. Nikolai had not sailed through these waters for about five years, and he had time to see how construction on both sides of the waterway had continued to expand dramatically. He took a few photos for his personal collection before they reached rather quieter waters and the Captain handed over "the con" to his new Lieutenant.

Nikolai was in command as the ships covered the hundred-plus miles through the Sea of Marmora, which was quite busy with oil tankers, freighters and cruise ships plying the sea lanes between the Black Sea and the Mediterranean. The three warships were a fairly unusual sight as they made their way southwards, in a line, at a steady 15 knots. Nikolai completed his watch, and eventually, they reached the Dardanelles, which meant another 100 miles of very busy shipping in the narrow channel between Europe and Asia, before sailing into the Aegean Sea.

And then the "cruise" was over. It was time for business in the Eastern Mediterranean. The three frigates were put on a battle-ready footing as they neared the Syrian coastline, and they began using their technology for the task of monitoring the American and European ships and submarines which were also operating in the area as a deterrent to President Assad's relentless attacks on the "rebel" groups in his country, supported by Russia. Then came a special duty when, for two days, the three frigates acted as "dummy targets" for Russian aircraft operating out of their Syrian base. This activity was all monitored and controlled from the sophisticated operations centre on board each ship.

To Nikolai and his fellow sailors, it seemed like the Cold War again, with long periods on high-level alert, until, after completing three intensive weeks in the area, their instructions changed. The captain announced that they would be heading westwards through the Mediterranean to eventually meet up with ships from the Russian Baltic fleet for a further period of exercises in the Atlantic Ocean.

It came as a welcome relief when they were no longer at "action stations" as they cruised towards their first stop, the dockyard in Malta, for refuelling and a few welcome days ashore to relax and explore the island. For many years, Valetta was the favourite watering hole for generations of British sailors, but it was now a more cosmopolitan port, and Russian sailors were just as welcome at the local bars, shops and clubs. It was also an opportunity for Nikolai to find an internet café where he was able to sign on to the dating website. From there he sent an e-mail to update on his travels to Marina: *"After a month at sea, we are now in Malta and heading your way."* Fortunately, she was on-line and was able to send an almost immediate reply:

"How lovely to hear from you again … It has been a long time, and I was becoming anxious. At last I know that you are really coming this way, and I look forward to seeing you. I have heard that Malta has a very interesting history, so bring some pictures. And let me know your date of arrival in Portsmouth." Which, of course, she already knew.

The "rest and recreation" stop was all too short for the crews of the three frigates, and soon they were setting off again, through the Straits of Gibraltar and into the Atlantic Ocean, to carry out a six-day programme of exercises with submarines from the Russian Baltic fleet. This enabled them to test their underwater electronics systems which seek and track the movement of submarines. It also meant more days and nights at "action stations" again, until the time came when fuel supplies had diminished, exactly as planned. But they still had sufficient reserves to cruise through the Bay of Biscay's winter storms and into the English Channel for their scheduled refuelling visit to Portsmouth Dockyard.

This is a traditional courtesy provided by most navies in the world in times of peace – though not often used because ocean-going refuelling tankers are usually available to work with operational ships as needed. But this time, the request for a refuelling stop from the Russian naval command to the British Ministry of Defence had been approved, not least because it would provide an opportunity for an up-close look at three of Russia's latest guided-missile warships.

As they sailed northwards, another few days ashore, this time in Portsmouth, were eagerly awaited by the Russian sailors – not least by Lieutenant Aldanov on board the *Admiral Essen*. Often, and especially on his long night watchkeeping duties, he found himself thinking about his first meeting with Marina.

3.
MARINA'S MOVE TO PORTSMOUTH

Marina's early life as an only child and at school in South London had been largely uneventful and generally happy. Her parents were occupied with their fabrics business, but family life was always a priority for them, and they never missed a school meeting for parents or a prize-giving event.

She made friends easily at primary school and retained strong friendships with childhood friends throughout her teenage and secondary school years. She was a popular student with an ever-packed schedule of after-school activities, and she enjoyed taking part in music and acting classes and theatre shows alongside her studies. In school, she was a studious girl with a flair for history and mathematics. She achieved a top grade for her GCSE mathematics and was put forward for the country's inter-school Senior Mathematics Challenge, where she achieved a gold certificate of excellence. Her teachers praised her natural mathematical abilities and suggested the prospect of her one day pursuing a career in accountancy or finance. These serious-sounding ideas felt a lifetime away for the teenage Marina, but she rather liked the idea of having a path laid out for her, and secretly enjoyed having something she was naturally rather good at. All in all, she was content to breeze through her A-Level examinations without too much stress.

With a strong set of results and a glowing academic reference from her tutors, Marina landed a place at Royal Holloway University in London to study accountancy. Her carefree school days were about to come to a sudden end as she moved into student halls of residence and embraced a round-the-clock timetable of seminars, lectures, all-night library sessions and endless essays and assignments. She took on a part-time job at the Student Union bar to help fund the ever-growing expenses of living in London and found herself enjoying the plunge into adulthood.

Whilst some of her peers and housemates frivolously ploughed through their student loan allowances within days of receiving them, Marina's mathematical mindset encouraged her to adopt strict budgeting and saving. She lived within her means during her University years, enjoying cheap Interrailing trips around Europe with friends during the summer holidays, and her horizons widened. She carefully put money aside for these adventures each month. She also longed to travel further afield – perhaps to Russia to bring to life some of her grandparents' fond memories – but for now, she was content to work, save and plan for a comfortable future.

She graduated with a 2:1 and was advised by the university to consider a career in the civil service. But jobs were not plentiful, and she was pleased to be offered a position in the finance department of a local London district council, which would make some use of her university training. It was a start, and her task was to maintain records of failures to pay council tax and start legal proceedings against miscreants. It was interesting, at least at first, and it paid the rent for the small flat which she shared with a former classmate in Dalston and left a little disposable income for general London life. Her long working weeks were punctuated by joining friends for a few drinks or the occasional date; although her social calendar was far from lavish, she was a social person by nature and really enjoyed her free time away from the office.

Her job at the council soon became routine and laborious, and although she was promoted to a supervisory role, she wished she had more room to develop and progress in the public sector. Some friends from her degree course had found accountancy jobs at big firms such as Goldman Sachs, and she couldn't help but feel a bit envious of their excessive pay cheques, exciting lifestyles and holidays. But she also saw these jobs in "the City" as somewhat insecure and risky.

She was always on the lookout for the right new opportunity and was scouring the recruitment websites when she spotted an advertisement from the Royal Navy. She had often pondered the excitement of working in the armed services, but truthfully, the prospect of long absences overseas did not appeal. However, this advertisement was for a civilian job, as an administrative assistant in the offices of the Commodore and based in Portsmouth Dockyard. It certainly ticked many of the right boxes for the next stage in her career. It was not too far from London, and the higher salary would mean an extra few hundred pounds each month to put away in her savings. Perhaps she would be able to upsize her flat or buy that new laptop she'd had her eye on? Her attention was most certainly caught. She was a quietly ambitious girl and not content to stay put in the same mediocre job for years on end, and so she bit the bullet and sent in an application. Somewhat to her surprise, she received a reply ten days later, inviting her to an interview in Portsmouth.

She did some online research and discovered that the Royal Naval Base in Portsmouth included the historic Portsmouth Dockyard, which was a tourist attraction, especially because it included Nelson's flagship, *HMS Victory*, from the Battle of Trafalgar in 1805. Also, there were the *Mary Rose* from Henry VIII's days, painstakingly salvaged from the Solent in recent years and now lovingly restored and on view to visitors, and *HMS Warrior*, one of the first ironclad ships from the 1860s, plus a naval museum. An exciting new life was beckoning … if all went well.

The day of the interview arrived, and Marina was feeling nervous as she followed the directions in her letter. From the Portsmouth railway station, she walked through the sights and sounds of a new environment, preparing to make her first acquaintance with the enticing world of the Royal Navy. After about 20 minutes, she walked through the historic Victory Gate into the Dockyard, showed her letter to a security guard and was directed to the offices of the Commodore. This was clearly visible from the gate, the tallest building in sight, topped by the new Semaphore Tower. The guard told her that this was where she would find the administrative functions of the Portsmouth naval command.

Once there, in good time for her appointment, she found an enquiries desk and absorbed her surroundings until, after a short wait, she was taken upstairs to the office of a female Navy officer, smartly uniformed and with two stripes on her arm. "Must be someone important," thought Marina as she took her seat across the desk as elegantly as she could. Although she was somewhat distracted by the view from the window of *HMS Victory*, the interview was relaxed and friendly and seemed to go smoothly. Afterwards, she was shown around the offices and, in particular, the Communications Department, where half-a-dozen desks were manned by civilian women staff, busy at their computers and wearing headsets. She was told that this was the hub of all the communications to and from the ships of the

Royal Navy's Portsmouth Base – currently over 40 surface ships in various parts of the world; the exception, it was explained, was the nuclear submarine fleet, which was a separate operation with communications handled elsewhere.

It was certainly something quite different for Marina and gave her much to think about on her train journey back to London. She had apparently made a good impression because early one morning a week later, she received a brown envelope bearing the initials OHMS – On Her Majesty's Service. She opened it carefully and pensively, and her heart leapt when she read the letter inside, offering her the job and at a salary well above her current earnings in London.

Her flatmate had already gone to work, and she could hardly wait to get to her office and share the news with her closest friends there. Then, in the evening, she went by underground train to visit her parents in Putney to tell them about her new opportunity. Her father, now semi-retired and quite Anglicised, was especially proud to hear of his daughter's new plans.

"Not just the navy, but the *Royal* Navy", he said over and over again to his wife Shona – who was pleased but also saddened by the prospect of her only daughter moving further away from them. "Your grandfather Viktor would never have believed it possible," he told them both. Then, turning to his daughter, he asked, "What will you be doing? Will you be on a ship?"

Marina explained, "Oh no, it's just an office job in the Dockyard. But when I went for my interview, it looked really interesting. It's in the section which handles all the communications between the headquarters and the various ships around the world. A bit different from chasing up unpaid council taxes."

"That sounds quite important, my dear, and I am sure you will do well. But come back to see us often, won't you?"

And they began to share her excitement as Marina went on to tell them all that she had learned so far about Portsmouth.

During the next month, while working out her notice period in her current job, she read all the research material she could find about Portsmouth and the Royal Navy. Searching on line, she also found herself a first-floor flat to rent in Southsea, just a ten-minute walk from the Dockyard. She phoned the rental agency and fixed a moving date for a few days before starting her new job and then found a "one man and a van" advertising in the local paper. She booked him to take her from London with her belongings to the new flat. It was just what she expected, small but comfortably furnished, with one bedroom and a nice enough view across Southsea Common towards the sea and the Isle of Wight in the distance.

"This will do very nicely," thought Marina, who was now in her thirtieth year, a tallish and elegant brunette but still single and preparing to adjust to a new phase in her life. After a quiet weekend of settling in and shopping for essentials, on the following Monday morning, she made the ten-minute walk to the Dockyard ready to start her new career.

She tried hard to hide her nervous feelings during that first day, which was a series of briefings and familiarisation tours. There were forms to be completed and documents to sign, including the Official Secrets Act, with all due solemnity in the presence of a senior officer. Then over the following days, after a spell of training with the department leader, she found her work in the communications office to be both challenging and all-consuming. During her working hours, she soon learned the fundamentals of the job, and her colleagues were friendly and helpful, often extending invitations for drinks in the evenings.

The time passed quickly, often making her forget her promise to visit her parents as often as she could. However, in recent times, she had often begun to question her current situation. What did the future hold? She had reached her thirties and was not really living the life she had hoped for. After more than two years in Portsmouth, she was still feeling lonely. Most of her colleagues went home to their husbands or boyfriends. This was what prompted her to try online dating sites – where she discovered Nikolai!

Was this to be the time when her ship would come home?

4.
"DOROGAYA"

Eventually, the big day came. It was about noon on a Wednesday when Marina stood on the sea wall, waiting for her first sighting of the visiting Russian ships. It was misty in the Solent area as she looked expectantly into the distance, past the four, dark grey, formidable stone Spithead sea forts dating from the Napoleonic wars. And then, at around the time she had expected, she spotted the small group of three ships appearing first as dots in the misty distance and then heading slowly in a line past the Isle of Wight and through the Spithead channel. She gave a tentative wave as the dark grey frigates passed her eager gaze and moved out of sight and into the harbour entrance.

She had not slept well, through anxiety perhaps, but the sea breeze had helped to awaken her spirits. She had taken the day off from work, and, with her mind spinning, she began to walk briskly towards the Dockyard. Along the way, she recalled the naval history of Portsmouth as she passed Battery Row and Sally Port, then the Cathedral so well restored after its bomb damage in World War Two. Then onwards to the impressively modernistic new development of Gunwharf Quay, with its shops and restaurants, and the soaring and dramatic feature of Spinnaker Tower, a symbolic feature visible from miles away.

Her walk took her along The Hard and past more historic landmarks such as the Keppels Head Hotel, from where the impressive stone and brick Dockyard gates came into view. As usual, the area was busy with coaches and tourists on their way to view the historic ships, and looming above it all was the towering building which housed the Commodore, his staff and the various administrative departments necessary to manage the work of the Dockyard.

In its heyday, the docks and jetties were usually full of naval ships, large and small, but the combination of defence cuts and modern naval operations meant there were now large spaces where once there had been aircraft carriers, cruisers, destroyers and minesweepers – either moored or undergoing maintenance in the dry docks.

Within an hour of arriving in the harbour, the three Russian ships had tied up safely alongside the South Railway Jetty – the place where the cruiser Ordzhonikidze had famously berthed when it brought the Soviet leaders, Bulganin and Khrushchev, to Britain on their official visit in 1956 for talks with Prime Minister Anthony Eden (and where the veteran frogman Commander "Buster" Crabb had lost his life in mysterious and controversial circumstances while trying to carry out a secret spying mission on the ship's propulsion system).

Marina was unaware of this piece of Portsmouth's naval history as she walked on through the activities of a still bustling dockyard, where tourists mingled with vehicles, dockyard workers and sailors. She found her way to the three Russian ships, and there, at long last, was the dark grey shape of *RS Admiral Essen*.

A uniformed Russian sailor was standing guard at the foot of the gangway and, in careful, simple English, she enquired about Lieutenant Nikolai Aldanov. He saluted politely as he recognised the name of one of his own officers and called to another sailor on deck. Marina waited, her heart thumping with a combination of excitement and anxiety, as the guard sent a messenger to find him.

After what seemed like a lifetime, she at last recognised her handsome officer in his smart, gold-braided uniform and peaked hat coming down the gangway to greet her. She had thought a hundred times about this moment and how she would welcome him – a hug, a handshake, even a kiss?

Nikolai took the initiative. He removed his uniform hat and tucked it under his arm, reached out to hold Marina's hand and kissed her on both cheeks. Then looking into her eyes, he said, in his perfect English with hardly a trace of an accent: "So here we are. Marina is a real person. This is wonderful."

Marina was suddenly speechless and overwhelmed, but pulled herself together to reply in a whisper: "Yes, here we are… I never thought this would really happen."

"Well it has," said Nikolai. "Let's stroll and have a chat."

He gently took her hand and as they walked along the jetty, watched by some envious sailors on board the Russian ship, he started telling Marina about their voyage from Sevastapol to Portsmouth.

The sailors were not the only ones watching them; in a discretely parked black car, two MI5 agents were also watching every move and taking photographs.

Nikolai spotted the nearby dock where the historic, first ironclad warship, HMS Warrior was moored, with a queue of tourists waiting to go on board. He asked about its history and this change of subject helped Marina to relax and she told him all about the famous 19th century ship. And she continued with the story of Nelson's flagship, HMS Victory when they could see her masts and flags further away in the Dockyard as they walked. Now regaining her composure, she asked: "How long will you be here?"

He explained that they were scheduled to refuel the Admiral Essen the next day and then sail for more exercises on the following day – but he added that he was not required to be on duty until the next morning and asked her, "So do you have time to show me a bit more of Portsmouth?"

Marina was pleased to say yes and pausing briefly to show him the office building where she worked, she explained that she had taken the day off, and added that as it was already mid-afternoon, they should make a start as soon as possible. Nikolai said he would need to change out of his uniform to "go ashore" and as they were walking past the Boathouse with its restaurants thronged with tourists, he suggested that she should wait for him there – "I will be back here in 10 minutes," he said, as he strode away.

Marina bought herself a cold drink and found a seat. She tried to think about where to take him – and in her mixed-up thoughts she suddenly wondered whether he would actually come back to find her? Also, since she did not have a car, they would be limited to places within reasonable walking distance.

And then Nikolai appeared at the door and searched anxiously among the groups of visitors. Marina saw him and waved. She thought he was looking specially handsome and very different in blue jeans and a grey, patterned sweater. As they met and he said warmly: "OK Marina, let's go."

They walked out through the Dockyard gates into The Hard where Marina pointed out the various features of the area including the famous Keppels Head Hotel, the Harbour railway station and the ferry service plying to and from Gosport where, she explained, there were several Royal Navy establishments. Then as they approached the modern development of the Gunwharf Quays shopping centre, she found herself rather naturally taking his arm as she guided him through the crowds toward the Spinnaker Tower. At the reception desk, she bought two tickets and they took the lift to the top deck where, from a height of 550 feet they had a dramatic view of the whole of Portsmouth and beyond to Southampton Water to the West, the Isle of Wight to the South with the Needles in the distance and the Sussex coast to the East. Marina had now lived in the area long enough to be able to give a commentary on all the views around them and to answer all of Nikolai's questions.

They took photographs of each other and asked another visitor to shoot photos of the two of them, posed and smiling happily with Nikolai's arm around his girlfriend.

"Wow," he said, finally. "This is amazing. I can even see my ship down there in the Dockyard. Show me where you live?"

Marina could easily point out the expanse of Southsea Common less than a mile away and the row of houses and apartments in the area, and she suggested that there was time to walk through that area and maybe find somewhere to have a meal together.

As they walked and talked, dusk was taking over on this autumnal evening and there was a full moon to watch, rising in a clear, darkening sky. In this more romantic atmosphere, they began to recall their on-line exchanges in which they had shared many personal thoughts and it seemed that the closeness they had felt in those impersonal contacts was being easily revived. Marina held Nikolai's arm ever more closely as she guided him through the streets of Portsmouth and pointed out the block of flats where she lived. They strolled on and into a nearby row of shops where she suggested they try an Italian restaurant.

There, they found a corner table (and did not spot the man who entered soon after and dined alone on a large pizza as he read the evening newspaper). As they sipped their prosecco, Marina and Nikolai began to discuss when and how they might meet again; and then over *linguini marinari* and a bottle of white wine, they talked about their past lives and about a time in the future when Marina might be able to visit the home of her ancestors in Russia. And as they held hands across the table, Marina asked: "What time do you have to be back on board your ship?" and Nikolai said, softly and meaningfully "Well, I am not on duty again until nine tomorrow morning."

Marina smiled and received the signal. "Let's skip dessert," she said softly. "And go back to my flat for coffee."

Nikolai asked for the check and paid for dinner with cash, explaining to Marina that the ship's officers had been paid in pounds sterling ahead of their arrival in Portsmouth to cover any personal expenses. And then, with their arms entwined, they strolled to the Southsea Terrace flats and Marina led the way into the lobby and then up to her first floor apartment – as quietly as possible without disturbing the neighbours.

Once inside, Nikolai took Marina in his arms and they kissed lovingly for the first time. After a minute or two, Marina came up for air and asked: "Coffee?" Nikolai replied briefly: "Later" – and he led her through the open door into what he had already spotted as the bedroom. There, they kissed repeatedly as they slowly undressed and sank eagerly on to the bed and spoke soft endearments to each other as they made love. While they kissed and caressed, each of them in their own way was also trying to assess the true depth of the feelings of the other until they were swept away in the intensity of the moment.

After a minute or two, a slightly breathless Nikolai moved away and murmured drowsily "*dorogaya, dorogaya.*" An elated Marina asked him: "That sounds nice; what does it mean?"

It means "my darling" he responded and then he appeared

to be dozing peacefully. Marina looked at him and quietly said to herself: "Can this really be true? This is what I have been dreaming of for years – a man who is loving and gentle and considerate…. and a handsome Russian, too … I wonder what happens next?"

Her meditations were suddenly disturbed by a ring of her doorbell. "Oh, surely not my neighbour at this hour," she said, pulling on a robe and walking into the sitting room, intending to look through the spyhole in the door. But before she could even get there, she heard the lock turning and in came two men in civilian clothes followed by a policewoman in uniform. As she reeled back, shocked by this sudden intrusion, the first man showed her his identity credentials as an agent with the Security Services and asked: "Is Nikolai Aldanov here?"

Alarmed and confused Marina spluttered an unintelligible answer as Nikolai appeared in the bedroom doorway, wrapped in a duvet, and asked: "What's going on?"

"Are you Nikolai Aldanov?" asked the agent.

"Who are you and why do you want to know?"

"My colleague and I are from the British Security Service and we have some questions for you to answer. It will be simplest if you get dressed quickly and come with us."

"I am an officer in the Russian Navy," replied Aldanov, trying hard to appear superior while in a state of undress and with his hair rumpled. "And I want to contact the captain of my ship in the Dockyard here before I do anything."

"You can do that from the police station", came the reply. "So let's go there quietly before we all disturb the neighbours here."

The second agent then led Aldanov back into the bedroom and watched him carefully while he dressed and as the two men led him out of the flat, he turned back to Marina and said: "Don't worry, my *dorogaya*. I will sort all this out and contact you later." They quietly took him down to a waiting car and drove off at speed. On the way, Nikolai was told abruptly to "shut up" when he asked, "Where are we going?" A few minutes later, the car arrived at the front door of the Portsmouth police station, and he was escorted into the building.

Meanwhile, the policewoman was still in the flat and carefully searching for anything left behind by the Russian. Marina interrupted and asked the her how they had managed to enter the front door and then her flat without making contact and was told: "These agents from London can do anything – even open locked doors. Now please get dressed. I am taking you to the police station because you also have some questions to answer."

"Me? What about?" asked Marina. "I haven't done anything wrong".

"You had better get dressed quickly and bring your toiletries too because you might be with us until tomorrow," said the policewoman, more sternly and looking at her watch. Then, dialling on her phone and waiting for a response, she said: "Are you still outside? OK, then we will be down in a few minutes."

Another police car was waiting outside and a bewildered Marina was escorted out of the building and into the back seats for the drive to the Portsmouth police station. By then, neighbours were at their front windows, watching these developments in amazement.

As the two cars each arrived at the police station just five minutes away, Marina and Nikolai were taken to separate interview rooms in the CID department, where waiting police officers asked them to empty their pockets, took away the contents and wrote notes to record their actions. They also took Marina's handbag, which contained, among other things, her mobile phone – ignoring her protest that she wanted to call her friend.

And the two lovers waited, separated, alone and confused – only hours after their first dockside meeting and their short, romantic evening together.

5.
INTERROGATION

"The Ruskies are very upset about whatever happened at Portsmouth yesterday," said Sir Oliver Anderson-Scott, a senior diplomat from the Foreign Office. "What's going on?"

He had been summoned to an early-morning meeting, hurriedly convened for 8 am at the Home Office, with representatives from the Security Services MI5, together with officials from MI6, the Ministry of Defence and Scotland Yard … and the story unfolded.

"It may be nothing special," began a calm and relaxed Thomas Spencer, a senior director from MI5. "This was just an opportunity to pick up a couple of suspected informants, and they are both being questioned in Portsmouth by our people. I should be able to tell you a lot more by tomorrow."

"Not good enough," said Sir Oliver, brusquely. "I am told that your people detained a Russian naval officer and a British woman not long after those visiting Russian ships arrived. The Russian Ambassador has already asked for the immediate release of the officer and diplomatic access to him before he is questioned. So, who are these people, and why were they detained? I need answers today, not tomorrow."

The MI5 man then explained that the Security Services had been monitoring internet communications between a woman working in the naval Commodore's HQ in Portsmouth and a Russian naval officer for several months and that they had become increasingly suspicious. The couple were using a popular dating website, but they had exchanged various references to naval activities in both Portsmouth and Sevastopol. The messages were currently being analysed by his department to establish the identity of the Russian and to discover whether there were any security breaches, possibly by sending information in a coded form.

Tom Spencer went on to explain that the website they were using was completely open and not protected in any way. But in the course of these online exchanges, the messages had discussed the visit by these Russian naval ships to Portsmouth and then a plan for the couple to meet, so they decided to track the movements of the woman and were ready to detain them at the first opportunity. He described how his agents had observed the couple when they met on the quayside in Portsmouth and had then tracked them as they visited various places in the city, eventually arriving at the woman's flat. Their conversations had been monitored from time to time, he said, including inside the flat, and although nothing incriminating was heard the decision was made to enter the flat late in the evening and detain them both for further questioning.

"So where are they now? And has anything leaked to the media about this incident yet?" asked Sir Oliver, in a firm voice.

"They have been at a Portsmouth police station overnight, with two of my people, and I am expecting a preliminary report very soon – and no, we are not aware of any press interest."

"Won't take long," barked Sir Oliver. "The police leak like a sieve, so be prepared. This incident will have to go up to the Minister as soon as I get back to the office, so let me know as soon as you have more information."

The officer from MI6 asked to be kept informed of any developments from the Russian angle and said he would liaise with their bureau in Moscow. The representative from the MoD said he was in touch with the Portsmouth Naval Command regarding the woman involved and that he would want to be told about in any inquiry relating to the operations in the Commodore's office. The man from Scotland Yard's anti-terrorism unit confirmed that the involvement by Portsmouth police was being carried out "by the book".

Spencer had been through this sort of thing many times before, taking care to include the many different parties with a special interest, and he knew that time was not on his side in making a decision about the next move. Was this a serious spying incident, which would involve Government ministers, or was it something trivial? Maybe even just a budding romance, in which case, over-reacting could prove embarrassing. The meeting broke up, with a plan to reconvene later in the day, and the participants went back to report to their respective departments on the story so far.

Spencer was soon on a direct phone link to his two experienced colleagues who had travelled to Portsmouth the previous day to handle the assignment. "What's the latest?"

He was told that the two suspects had been held overnight at the police CID department and were being questioned separately to establish as many facts as possible. Neither of them had yet been cautioned or charged, but they had confirmed that the woman worked in a sensitive part of the Commodore's office in the Dockyard. A senior naval officer there had just been informed of the woman's whereabouts, but they had not shared any details at this stage about the reasons for her absence from work.

The MI5 officers also reassured their chief that they had remembered to ask the police inspector on night shift to

The Russian Lieutenant

bring in the local on-call solicitor "just in case". They said that a somewhat dishevelled man called Jeremy Scott had arrived to go through the appropriate legal instructions separately with the two detainees, advising each of them that they were entitled to say "no comment" in reply to any questions they were asked, and to request a break if they felt too tired to continue. The agent added that the Russian detainee appeared to understand English but was refusing to say anything until he had an interpreter and an officer from his ship or someone from the embassy with him. The woman was being hysterical at times and asking to talk to her boss in the Dockyard office, insisting that she had done nothing wrong. When asked, she had confirmed that in her online exchanges with her "date", she had told him about her own Russian ancestry.

In their verbal report, the two agents went on to describe to Tom Spencer how, after two sessions of interviews with the couple about their past history, their special interests, and their friends and contacts, they had built up the profiles – more successfully with Marina Peters than with the Russian. They had decided that everyone needed a break soon after midnight and the local police team had set up camp beds with blankets for the detainees in the two interview rooms.

Some seven hours later, and after providing some breakfast of coffee and pastries, the two agents said they had continued their interrogation of the two individuals who were still being held in separate rooms. They had started on the next stage of the interviews, which was to try to establish how the relationship had come about and what each of them knew about the other. This was still in progress, they said, when this call came from their boss in London.

Tom listened carefully to their report, without interrupting, and then replied, "That sounds fine, so far. Let me have a written summary of your sessions to date as soon as possible – send it over on the usual link to my tablet. And get the CID people there to take a photo of each of them and have them transmitted to my office. But take care not to ruffle the Russian feathers too much at this stage. There's already a problem at the Foreign Office, so ease off the pressure until I get back to you."

The call ended, and the two agents decided to take a break from questioning to prepare the written report on progress while they awaited further instructions from London.

6.
THE TIP-OFF!

At about the same time, early on this Thursday morning, Gary Andrews was in his small bachelor flat in Fratton, trying to sleep off a heavy night down at his local pub, when his phone rang. He was the crime reporter at the Portsmouth Herald, and it was not unusual for him to be disturbed at inconvenient moments. This time it was one of his contacts at the police station.

"Sorry to call you so early," Gary heard through his hazy brain. "It's Bill here – are you OK? Look, there's something a bit odd going on here this morning. Some plainclothes people we haven't seen before brought in a bloke last night who looked like a foreign naval type, and there was a woman with him. I have been told that they have been questioning them here all night. Just thought there might be something in it for you."

"Thanks, Bill – I'll check around. Let me know if you hear any more."

After grabbing a quick breakfast, Gary drove his small Fiat to his parking slot at the newspaper office in the town centre and soon found the paper's naval correspondent at his desk. He asked him casually, "Any foreign ships in port that you know of?"

"Yes, I did a piece last night," said Charles Williams.

"There are three Russian frigates in the Dockyard – came in from some exercises in the Med. My contacts said they are probably here to get fuel before going on to join their Baltic Fleet friends. Not often we see them here, but it's happened before... Seems just routine. Why do you ask?"

Gary told him about his early-morning tip-off, and Charles said he would go straight to the Dockyard and call on his usual contacts to see what might be going on. If it is a foreign sailor at the police station, he conjectured, it might just be connected with the Russian visitors. In any case, he wanted to get a photo or two of the Russian ships to illustrate the story he was writing for Friday's edition.

Meanwhile, Gary set off for his regular morning visit to the police station to take a look at the occurrences log for the past 24 hours with the duty sergeant. As usual, there were a couple of arrests of drunken sailors, a domestic row out in the suburbs and a fairly serious road accident – two injuries. All seemed normal – except that as he walked outside, his eagle eye spotted an unfamiliar black 4 x 4 vehicle in the car park at the front of the building with a London registration. It also had a more-sophisticated-than-usual radio antenna.

Gary returned to the police sergeant's desk and enquired, casually, "Has the Chief Constable got a smart new vehicle, then?"

"No idea, pal," replied the sergeant. "Saw it myself when I came in this morning, and CID told me it was a bit hush-hush – can't say any more."

Gary's journalistic instincts immediately sensed something a bit fishy. As he went back through the car park, he surreptitiously took a quick picture of the black car on his mobile phone and then drove back to the newspaper office deep in thought. Who drives a vehicle like that? Must be something or someone special? And if that foreign naval type came from the Dockyard, he could have something to do with the Russian ships. Ah yes, Russians – that could be a story…?

Back in the newsroom, he was just doing some online research about the Russian navy when Charles called him from the Dockyard.

"Something is going on here," he said. "They are not saying anything in the information office about the Russian ships except that they are scheduled to leave at the weekend. But when I was taking my pictures, one of the Dockyard foremen working nearby told me that soon after the ships docked yesterday, he saw a strange car pull up at the dockside and one of the men in the car took photographs as one of the Russian officers came down the gangway and met a woman who appeared to be waiting for him."

"Did he say what sort of car?"

"I'm not far away," said Charles. "I'll go back and ask him – hold on."

Gary overheard the conversation. "Yeah. I think it was a big black job," said a third voice. "It was one of those four-wheel drives – don't see many of those around here."

Gary interrupted. "Charles, ask him what happened next and if he saw where the couple went?"

"I was quite a long way away", came the reply. "But the officer and the woman walked off into the Dockyard and I think one of the men from the car was following them."

Back in the newsroom, Gary and Charles put their heads together and spent the next hour calling their various police and naval contacts to see if there were any more clues. The next clue came when a friend of Charles', who worked as transport manager in the Dockyard offices, told him that there was certainly some unusual activity going on. A couple of senior officers had arrived in the past half hour for an unscheduled meeting "upstairs with the bosses". The office gossip was that they were making enquiries about one of the women in the communications department who had not arrived for work as usual, and they had asked several of her colleagues in the offices if they knew how to contact her.

"What's her name?" asked Charles.

"Give me five minutes. I think I know who to ask. I'll go somewhere quiet and call you back soonest," came the reply.

The call came just a few minutes later. "Apparently, they're looking for someone called Marina Peters – she lives in Southsea Terrace."

Charles and Gary decided that it was time to brief their editor, Matthew Sampson. He was upstairs, sitting behind his traditional walnut desk, reading the morning papers, as they knocked on the door and went into his office. They soon got his full attention as they each outlined what they knew at this stage, and he advised them to be cautious; there were not many facts to go on yet, he pointed out. He, too, could smell a rat as they began to put the pieces together, but he also knew his responsibilities if an emerging news story involved the police, the Navy, the Russians and a mysterious black car from London.

"Let me make a few calls," he said. "And you can send one of the young reporters over to Southsea Terrace to find out anything he can about Miss Peters; don't tell him why – he can make up an excuse."

The editor's first call was to the Portsmouth Police Chief Constable, Terence Hardy – they were on good terms and had belonged to the same local golf club for years. He had the Chief's direct line phone number, and it had been their understanding that they could always exchange information in confidence.

"Sorry to bother you, Terence," he began. "It's not about my nomination to the golf club committee this time. It's about a story my guys have got wind of today. Something about a foreign naval officer brought in for questioning … and they think it may have something to do with the Russian ships in the Dockyard. Should I be interested?"

"Can't say a thing, Matthew – you know I would if I could, but there are other parties involved, and I hope you will tell your guys to leave it alone at the moment. I will give you a call as soon as I know more. Okay?"

"Yes, understood. I'll stay in touch."

The editor could read between the lines. There was clearly something going on, and he suspected that if Russians were involved, it might have some national security angle which he would need to handle very carefully. Next, he called the office of the Royal Navy Commodore in the Dockyard and asked to speak to the number two man, Commander Robert Gaffney, who had been serving there for quite a few years and was experienced in dealing with the Press on confidential naval matters; he was also well known in Portsmouth dining circles. But he was not available, even for his friend Matthew, and neither was anyone else. "Try again later in the day," was the unusual response from a junior officer. Matthew was not often rebuffed by his personal network.

Meanwhile, the young reporter had returned from the flat in Southsea Terrace with the news that Miss Peters had not been seen there since the previous day – but he went on to tell Gary that he had spoken to one of the elderly residents who told him that she had been surprised to be woken up by a police car arriving early that morning. She had then seen two police officers come into the building, and somehow they had entered Marina's flat and spent about half an hour inside before leaving with several boxes.

And that was not all, the reporter added. She also said there had been "something funny" going on late the previous evening and she had heard comings and goings and had looked out and seen a police car there as well. The neighbour was understandably very concerned and had been trying without success to contact the only friend of Marina's she knew; she gave the Herald reporter the name and phone number of one Betty McGuire.

Gary returned upstairs again and reported these latest developments to the editor. They called Charles into the office again for another review of the situation. The Herald had had a fine reputation as an evening newspaper for many years, but because of commercial pressures, it was no longer published daily. Since it was now Thursday morning and the next edition of the weekly paper would be put together that day for publication on Friday, they had limited time to think.

They pondered and decided that Gary should next try to find this Betty McGuire while Charles kept an eye on the Dockyard and his naval contacts, and they would meet again mid-afternoon to hopefully finalise the story for that week's edition.

Gary checked the voter register and discovered that Betty and her husband lived in a new block of flats off Arundel Street. He called her number but got no reply. He decided not to leave a voicemail message but to try the address anyway. As he drove through the city, he did some more pondering about another dilemma. His best drinking friend, Mike Morrissey, was the local freelance reporter and correspondent for most of the London national newspapers – and they *always* swapped information on the stories they were covering. Mike's tip-offs sometimes helped Gary to shine with exclusive stories that pleased the editor of the Herald; Gary often heard titbits which Mike could develop into a story for the London tabloids – and also paid for a few drinks. But should he share this emerging story – which might turn out not to be a story at all? Or it could be something big. Should he wait 24 hours so that the Herald could feature an "exclusive"? Or perhaps it would help to let the experienced Mike loose on the story…

He decided to wait a bit longer, and when he arrived at the Arundel Street flats, neighbours told him that Betty was a nurse, working shifts at the local hospital, and that she came home at unusual times. Her husband worked in a High Street furniture store, and just as he was sitting back in his car, working out which direction to try next, Gary spotted a woman in nurse's uniform walking towards the flats from the bus stop. His lucky day?

He followed her to the door and, as politely as he could, asked, "Excuse me, but are you Betty McGuire?"

"Who wants to know?"

"I'm Gary Andrews from the Herald. I am very sorry to bother you, but may I have a few words – it's about your friend Marina."

"What's happened to her? Come on in for a moment," she replied anxiously.

When they got inside and Betty had taken off her coat and sat down in the kitchen, Gary explained that Marina had not turned up for work as expected that morning. He said the Navy had asked the police to make some enquiries, and it was quite normal for the local paper to follow up this sort of thing in case someone else knew something. Someone like Betty, for example.

"When did you last talk to Marina?" Gary asked.

"At the weekend – we usually see each other somewhere at the weekend unless I am working overtime. On Sunday, we went for a walk on the seafront and had a cup of tea at her flat. Why, what has happened?"

"Nothing I know of yet," said Gary. "Did she have any other special friends who could help me – like a boyfriend or anything?"

"I don't think there is anyone special at the moment, but

she was a bit excited about a fellow she had met on one of those dating sites on-line. She didn't say a lot, that was her way. But I think she said he was a foreign naval bloke and she was expecting to meet him when his ship arrived this week. Single girls here in Portsmouth do a lot of that, but I know Marina was always very careful about meeting strangers – especially sailors. Would you like a cup of tea?"

"Not at the moment, thanks, but that's really helpful," said Gary, now trying anxiously to get away without looking rude. "I don't suppose you have a picture of Marina I could borrow, do you?"

Betty went through to her bedroom and came back with a framed picture. "That's the two of us in the Dockyard at the Navy Days last year – it's the best one I've got."

"Tell you what, Betty. Could I just borrow it for a couple of hours and then return it to you, please?"

And with a few more pleasantries, Gary made his exit as quickly as he could and probably broke a few driving regulations on his way back to the office.

"It's coming together," he said, breathlessly to the editor. He went on to report on his conversation with Betty McGuire and showed him the photograph. He then took the photograph down to the art department with instructions to make several copies, deliver them all to him and then find someone to take the original "in exactly the same state" back to the owner. He scribbled Betty's name and address on a slip of paper.

7.
"A RUSSIAN SPY?"

Gary did not need to be so concerned about his "exclusive". Not long after his early-morning wake-up call, his freelance friend Mike Morrissey had also received a call. This was from *his* local police contact, who was a detective working in the CID; he, therefore, knew much more about the events there during the night than Gary's friend Bill. He spilled out the information that a Russian naval officer and a Portsmouth woman who worked for the Royal Navy were being questioned by two men who had come to Portsmouth the previous day from MI5 in London. They were still there.

Mike quickly made some more calls but was not able to get any confirmation from his usual contacts in the Dockyard, other than details about the three Russian naval ships which had arrived the previous afternoon. "Just a fairly routine refuelling stop for 24 hours," he was told. When asked, his contact added that it was not often that the Russian Navy visited Portsmouth these days.

Mike trusted his police contact, and this sketchy information was enough for him to put two and two together and call his best Fleet Street contact, David Hancock, the news editor at the Daily Star in London. He knew they would pay the most for an exclusive story, especially one involving MI5, the Russians – and a woman! Mike outlined the details he knew so far and then followed up by e-mail with a few more facts, such as where the ships were berthed and the exact location of the police station. Hancock wasted no time in getting things moving. He briefed two of his reporters to follow up with their contacts at the Home Office, at the Foreign Office and with Scotland Yard's National Security section, and then he despatched one of his best men to drive immediately to Portsmouth to work with Mike Morrissey.

The contacts made by the Daily Star reporters in London during the morning led to a flurry of phone calls between government departments. Ministers were informed, and this activity led to another urgent background briefing at the Home Office, who were taking the initiative, since at this stage, it was essentially a police and MI5 matter. The decision was made to bring the Russian officer from Portsmouth to London as soon as possible for further interrogation. At the same time, they would move cautiously with the woman and continue to process her involvement locally in Portsmouth. The MoD would liaise with the Portsmouth naval command, and meanwhile, the Foreign Office would keep the Russian Embassy informed.

Word had quickly spread that the press was onto it and, by early afternoon, the Foreign Office had issued a statement which went out to all the usual newspaper, news agency and broadcasting editors:

"Following the arrival of three frigates of the Russian Navy for refuelling in Portsmouth yesterday, it proved possible to follow up a long-term security operation by MI5 relating to an exchange of information between a member of the ship's company of RS Admiral Essen (one of the three frigates) and a staff member in the offices of the Commodore of the Portsmouth Royal Navy Base. The two

people concerned were detained for questioning by the Security Service, and further investigations are taking place. The names will be released later. The Ambassador of Russia to the United Kingdom has been informed."

Meanwhile, in Portsmouth, Mike contacted his friend Gary at the Herald. He discovered that he was already on the story, and they agreed to compare notes. Mike then went to meet the staff reporter from the Daily Sta*r,* who had just arrived in Portsmouth, and briefed him as far as he could. They went to a pub to meet Gary, and as they exchanged information, they quickly recognised that this story was becoming *big*. They were particularly impressed when Gary produced a copy of the photograph he had borrowed, and this was quickly scanned and sent to the Daily Star head office in London.

By the end of the day, the Daily Star had enough facts for a front-page splash in Friday's paper. It was a story with the by-line of their Security Correspondent, together with the photo of Marina and Betty, and with the bold headline:

A RUSSIAN SPY? OR JUST A DATE?
MI5 detains Royal Navy woman at a Dockside tryst

WHEN A PORTSMOUTH WOMAN MET A VISITING SAILOR IN PORTSMOUTH ON WEDNESDAY, TWO MI5 AGENTS INTERRUPTED THEIR TRYST AND TOOK THEM TO THE LOCAL POLICE STATION FOR QUESTIONING. THE WOMAN WORKS IN THE NAVY HQ IN THE DOCKYARD, AND THE SAILOR HAD ARRIVED EARLIER IN THE DAY ON BOARD A RUSSIAN WARSHIP.

NO NAMES HAVE BEEN RELEASED, BUT THE WOMAN HAS BEEN IDENTIFIED BY HER NEIGHBOURS AS MARINA PETERS AND IS REPORTED TO BE SINGLE, AGED ABOUT 30, AND HAS WORKED AT THE DOCKYARD FOR ABOUT THREE

YEARS (photo shows Marina on the left with her friend Betty McGuire at the Portsmouth Navy Day earlier this year).

A STATEMENT FROM THE FOREIGN OFFICE CONFIRMED THAT THE RUSSIAN HAD ARRIVED IN PORTSMOUTH ON BOARD THE FRIGATE RS ADMIRAL ESSEN, AND THAT THE WOMAN WORKED IN THE ROYAL NAVY COMMODORE'S OFFICE IN PORTSMOUTH. THEY WERE "DETAINED FOR QUESTIONING" AS PART OF A LONG-TERM SECURITY OPERATION BY MI5.

THE FOREIGN OFFICE SAID THE RUSSIAN AMBASSADOR HAD BEEN INFORMED AND THAT FURTHER INVESTIGATIONS WERE TAKING PLACE.

THE ADMIRAL ESSEN IS ONE OF THREE NEW RUSSIAN FRIGATES WHICH ARRIVED IN PORTSMOUTH TO REFUEL DURING EXERCISES IN THE ATLANTIC. THIS IS A RARE VISIT BUT IS DESCRIBED BY NAVAL EXPERTS AS "A COURTESY BETWEEN NAVIES IN MANY COUNTRIES."

(SPY FLASHBACK! THESE RUSSIAN SHIPS ARE MOORED AT THE SAME JETTY WHERE ANOTHER FAMOUS SPY INCIDENT OCCURRED IN 1956. THAT WAS WHEN THE CRUISER ORDZHONIKIDZE BROUGHT THE SOVIET LEADERS KHRUSCHEV AND BULGANIN TO BRITAIN AND THE NAVY FROGMAN COMMANDER "BUSTER" CRABB MADE HIS FATAL ATTEMPT TO SPY ON THE UNDERWATER EQUIPMENT OF THE SHIP.)

8.
OFFICIAL SECRETS ACT

At the Portsmouth Police Station on Thursday morning, the Chief Constable and his head of CID were assessing the implications of the major situation which had suddenly descended on them. They were concerned that on MI5 and Scotland Yard instructions, they had now detained the two individuals overnight as a security inquiry and were trying to decide what to do next. They were relieved when one of the MI5 officers came into the office to tell them that after discussions with his boss, they were planning to leave for London shortly with the Russian officer.

Then he added, "But it will be your job to take further statements from the woman we detained and to make a decision on when it is appropriate to release her on bail – pending further inquiries, of course. There is not enough evidence to charge her with anything at present, but we suggest you keep an eye on her and give her a warning about not talking to the press or anyone else about it."

He also asked them to interview her Navy bosses to establish whether she had signed the Official Secrets Act and to find out what confidential information she might have been aware of. Then he said, almost as an afterthought, "By the way, be a bit careful – she has a Russian background herself – she used to be Marina Petrov."

This unexpected news certainly got the attention of the two senior Portsmouth Police officers. They sat upright in their chairs and looked at each other knowingly, both thinking what the CID Chief then said: "Wow – this is now a whole new ball game!" As he left and said goodbye, the MI5 man added, "And by the way, say nothing to the press about this – if they get wind of the detention of the Russian, just say that there will be a statement from the Foreign Office in due course."

Left on their own, Matthew Sampson then told his CID chief, Paul Maggs, about the call he had received earlier from the editor of the Herald. "We've got a problem – the cat is already out of the bag. I don't know how they heard about it, but we can't put it back in now! I think you had better go down to join the London guys now and see them off with their Russian – and then follow up with this woman. What's her name now?"

Detective Superintendent Maggs, informed him: "Well, her English name is Marina Peters," and he went off to set up the arrangements for the formal interview with her. But first, in the CID department, the two men from MI5 gave him a quick summary of their meetings during the night and then prepared to leave with the Russian, who was still protesting and now looking even more unkempt.

The Chief Constable then placed another call to the Navy Commodore's office. This time, he reached Commander Gaffney, who said he had been expecting the call and thanked him for the earlier message when an officer who said he was from London had explained the absence of the staff member from the Communications Office. Told that the lady concerned was being interviewed at the police station on a security matter and that the press were already making inquiries, Gaffney said this was a worrying development and he had no idea how the story had leaked and continued: "I've already heard from the MOD that this now also a matter for MI5 and the Foreign Office because it involves a Russian national, and that the FO will be issuing a statement later today. We are bound to get more inquiries from the press because an official statement will go to all the usual places. Will that help you?"

"The sooner the better," replied the Chief Constable. "Will you be dealing with any press inquiries about this woman Peters? She is still here at the station for questioning, but she has not been charged with any offence at this stage. We've already had a call from the local paper, and we still have to decide what to do with her… Can you tell me any more? Has she been there long, and was she doing any secret or confidential work?"

"We've had no problems with her since she joined us," continued the Commander. "She is a bright and intelligent lady, from what I know. What does she do? Well, she's in the department which handles all the comms traffic between us and the Admiralty – ship movements, future plans and so on. Sorry, I'm an old-timer, and I still call it the Admiralty instead of the MOD… and all the staff here have to sign the Official Secrets Act, of course. And I really have no idea what the link is with the Russian fellow except that I assume it is connected with the three frigates which arrived yesterday. I guess your MI5 guys will know more about that."

"Thank you, Robert, we are all working on it," replied Matthew. "And by the way, did you know that Miss Peters used to be Miss Petrov and has a Russian family background?"

There was a moment's silence. "Can't say I did, old man. But I suspect it's all in her files – or I hope it is. Goodbye for now."

Downstairs in the CID's interview room, Detective

Superintendent Maggs, with one of his bright young detective sergeants, was ready to start their formal questioning of Marina Peters. After her late-night session with MI5, she had managed to get a few hours' rest. She had been taken to the ladies' cloakroom by a policewoman for an opportunity to freshen up and was offered a bacon sandwich and coffee brought up from the staff canteen. The solicitor, Jeremy Scott, had returned early and accompanied Marina when she went into the interview room again.

"Do you know why you are here, Miss Peters?" Maggs began, in his best attempt at a friendly voice.

"Not really," she replied quietly. "May I speak to my supervisor at the office?"

"Not at the moment, I'm afraid, but they know you are here. Now, you have not been charged with any offence, so there is no need to caution you. And I know you are tired and upset after an all-night session here, so I will try to keep this as easy for you as I can. Mr. Scott, your solicitor here, will give you any help and advice you may need if you are in any doubt. But first, may I ask you how well you know this Russian navy officer called Nikolai Aldanov?"

Marina turned to the solicitor. "Shall I answer?" He nodded.

"Well, hardly at all. He was just a face on a dating website, and we got into the habit of chatting from time to time – there's nothing wrong with that."

"No, of course not, "said Maggs. "But you must understand that it is a bit unusual for someone in an important job with the British navy to start exchanging information with an officer in the Russian Navy. Did you not think of that?"

"No, not in that sense," she replied. "It was just that he looked nice and we seemed to have some interests in common and we began to get to know each other better, in stages."

"You spent quite a lot of time together yesterday. What did you talk about?"

"It was the first time we had met in person," Marina replied, rather coyly. "We just had so much to catch up on and I think we both realised that we had become really close, in spite of being at such a distance until now. It really seemed like we had known each other for ages, which of course we had."

"Did you tell him that your grandparents came from Russia?"

The solicitor whispered to her, "You don't have to answer that."

But Marina replied, "It's not a secret, and it gave us an interesting subject to talk about."

"Did it make you feel you were both on the same side, as it were?" asked Maggs.

The solicitor, warming now to the importance of his task, and in spite of a sleepless night, intervened and suggested quietly that she should refuse to say anything further at this stage. She appeared to agree, so he said to the detectives, "Unless you have any further matters, I think Miss Peters needs a rest."

Maggs turned to his sergeant and said, "Right. I think that is all we need for now. So would you arrange for Miss Peters to be released on conditional bail and make sure we know how to get in touch with her if we need to? And find a driver to take the young lady home."

She began to feel relieved, but before she left, he added rather sternly, "Please remember that, because of your job, you signed the Official Secrets Act, so be very, very careful what you say to anybody. That includes your friends and particularly the press. And by the way, we have been to your flat and now have your laptop computer and mobile phone here. We will get someone to return them by tomorrow. Thank you, Miss Peters, and goodbye for now."

The young solicitor interjected and asked: "Can you just go to Miss Peters' flat and take her computer like that without a warrant?"

"It was done correctly, Mr. Scott; this is a national security matter," came the instant reply. On the way out, the solicitor handed his card to Marina and told her to ring him later to discuss the next steps. He advised her again not to talk to anyone else about the events of the past 24 hours, especially the press.

She paused at the door and turned back to the CID chief. "Where's Nikolai?"

"I'm sorry, but I can't tell you that," replied Superintendent Maggs. "And by the way, you can collect your handbag on the way out, but we need to keep your mobile phone a bit longer. We will return it with your laptop as soon as we can. Oh, and you should ring your father in London. He has called your mobile a couple of times this morning."

"Did you speak to him?" asked Marina. And when he told her they did not answer the calls, she said, "Then how did you know it was him?"

Maggs replied, "His number was on the phone as the caller."

Marina, still hovering in the doorway, was alert by now and asked, "How did you know it was his number?"

"We know everything," said the CID chief as he finally walked out. "We will be in touch with you again as soon as possible, and maybe by tomorrow I will know more."

A kindly woman police officer arrived and escorted Marina to the lobby where she collected her handbag. They went down to a police car in the underground car park and drove her back to Marina's flat at about noon.

Marina took her door keys from her handbag – and suddenly realised that the police must have used them to get into her flat earlier. Using the security code, she opened the door into the lobby and took the lift to the first floor. She used her key to open the door and entered gingerly, but everything appeared to be normal, except that her laptop was missing from her desk and it had been disconnected from her printer. As she looked around, she began to think of a myriad of questions about what she should do next. She must call her father straight away. Who could she contact to find out what had happened to Nikolai? Her solicitor perhaps? And what about her job? She could not e-mail anyone without her laptop. Then her landline phone rang, and it was Betty.

"There you are at last," she said. "I have been worried since the press came to see me this morning to find out if I knew where you are? I thought you were missing and gave them a photograph to help them find you. What's happened? I must come over to have a chat and see how you are."

"I am very tired and all mixed up," said Marina. "I've been with the police since yesterday afternoon – I need a sleep, so can you make it later in the day?"

"Of course, if that's best for you, I will. Look, I'm on duty tonight, so I will pop in on my way. I'll give you a call first… but aren't you going back to work?"

"I don't know what I am doing yet. You've reminded me that I had better call the office to find out if they know anything. Do I even still have a job? I'll let you know later."

Marina wandered round the flat aimlessly. She tried to call her father, but his phone line was busy. She found she had some milk in the refrigerator and made herself a cup of tea – there were a few biscuits in the tin – then she found some bread to make toast. After another snack, she tried again to reach her father.

"Hello, my dear Marina. I am so worried about you," he began, in his still-accented English. "Where have you been? You have not answered your mobile. Are you all right?"

"Yes, I think so, Pa," she said. "It's a long story, and I don't know where to begin. It's all because I have been chatting to a Russian sailor on my computer and this has created a bit of a stir and the police are investigating. But don't worry. I'll try to see you over the weekend and tell you everything. But don't talk to anyone, please, because I think the press may want to find out about it. They have already contacted my friend Betty."

"But who is this Russian fellow?" asked Victor. "Is this why I just had a call from the Russian embassy this morning, wanting to come to see me? Why me? I don't know anything…."

Marina's head was spinning.

"I'll call you again later, Pa, when I've had a rest, and give my love to Mum," she said and went slowly to her bedroom. Why did the Russian embassy contact her father, she wondered? She lay down and fell into a deep sleep almost instantly.

She was woken when the phone rang, and then the external doorbell buzzed insistently. She looked at the time, and it was only four o'clock. She had slept for less than three hours and decided to ignore the callers. Then peering cautiously around her curtained front window, she could see three cars parked outside. A small group had gathered down below at the front of her block of flats.

She quickly guessed that it was the press. In fact, reporters from the national and local press had started descending on Portsmouth following the Foreign Office statement. Radio and TV reporters and cameramen were there, too – and although there was no confirmation about Marina's involvement, Mike Morrissey had passed on her address to the visiting reporters (and knew he would get a fee for his information). Mike had been given the address by Gary, and the two of them were the first ones there that afternoon. When they got no reply from the call button for her flat, they spoke to her neighbours as they came and went but could discover very little useful information. Just a few snippets …

"Yes, we know Marina … been here two or three years … a lovely lady … very friendly … single, we think … works for the Navy in the Dockyard … haven't seen her for a day or two … goes off sometimes to her family in London … don't think she has a special boyfriend." And then, from one or two of the neighbours, came the unanswered question: "Why do you want to see her?"

As more reporters arrived, Gary agreed to take a couple of them to Betty's flat, only to discover when they arrived that Marina's friend had gone out. He told them she was a nurse at the local hospital, and they all went off to the hospital in search of her, but without success.

Another group of reporters was 'camped out' with their TV cameras at the police station and they learned that a photographer from the Herald had been there that morning in time to get a distant shot of the big black car leaving with a man thought to be the Russian in just visible in the back seat, accompanied by a driver and one other man in the back of the car. Their bosses in London were soon calling the Herald to buy rights to this first important picture. When Marina was driven out later, she was unseen as the unmarked vehicle emerged from an underground car park at the rear of the police station.

There was still no statement or interview forthcoming from the Chief Constable or CID chief during the afternoon – only the brief facts in the statement from the Foreign Office. It was the same at the Dockyard, where no-one at the Commodore's office was willing to be interviewed. Facts were scarce. But from the public part of the Dockyard, the three Russian ships could be seen moored at the jetty, providing the background for a TV reporter to introduce his report to camera for the evening news:

"This is where the mystery of the Russian naval officer began yesterday afternoon. As he came ashore from one of those three ships behind me, the Admiral Essen, he met a woman who it is believed was waiting for him on the dockside. Plain clothes police were watching their movements and later in the day they were both detained at a flat in nearby Southsea. Since then, they have both been at a Portsmouth police station. According to local sources, they are still there and have been interviewed by officers who arrived by car from London, thought to be from MI5…."

9.
THE LAWYER

Marina felt trapped in her flat and badly needed advice on what she should do next. She had another short conversation with her father and a reassuring chat with her mother. Then she rang her supervisor's number at the Dockyard offices and had to leave a message. She called Betty and advised her not to come to the apartments because of the posse of reporters waiting at the door. She decided to give Betty a few more facts about the reasons for the press and police interest and her online friendship with a Russian. Betty was, in turn, alarmed and sympathetic, and they agreed to stay in touch.

Marina thought she should switch on her TV. She found the 24-hour news channel and was shocked to see that the Portsmouth "spy story" was the headline news. She was even more alarmed to suddenly see a live report coming from outside her own flat. It was an out-of-world experience that made her head spin again. And then she jumped with fright as there came a knock on her door.

She relaxed a little when she peeped through the eye-hole and saw it was her friendly but elderly neighbour, Mrs. Watkins. She quickly let her inside.

"I didn't know you were here," she said, "but then my next-door neighbour told me she thought she saw you come home in a police car, so when I could just hear that your TV was on, I thought I had better come in to see if you are all right."

"Thank you so much," said Marina. "Let me switch off the TV … it is so good of you because I am being a nuisance to everyone with these reporters outside and ringing the doorbells. I am so sorry.…"

"I don't want to pry," said Mrs. Watkins, "but I don't really understand what is going on. Why are they all here? Can I make us a cup of tea?"

She went to Marina's kitchen to make two mugs of tea and when they sat down, Marina began to explain. "You have probably heard about these websites on the computer where you can make new friends. Well, it all began when I made contact with a very nice man who turned out to be an officer in the Russian navy. He seemed very friendly and when he said his ship was visiting Portsmouth, I agreed to meet him. You know I work in the Dockyard offices, don't you? Well, I knew when this ship was arriving and went to try to find him yesterday. When he came ashore, we met up and decided to spend the day together looking around the city and we came back here for coffee. Then suddenly, the police were here and they took us both away to the police station. And I never saw him again."

She started to cry and sipped her tea as Mrs. Watkins thought for a few moments. "I don't really understand all this computer stuff, so perhaps you will show me one day. But don't get upset. I'm sure it will all work out all right. Things usually do, you know."

Marina then continued: "Well, the police asked me over and over again last night and today about why I was meeting him and how much I knew about him – so he must have been involved in something I didn't know about. They refused to tell me what it was. I got a bit upset, and it was all very tiring, and they didn't let me come home until midday today. Actually, that reminds me that they did get me a young solicitor to advise me. I think I had better ring him soon to find out what I should do next."

"Well, my dear, you weren't to know, were you?" said Mrs. Watkins. "All that must be why I had a young reporter from the Herald here earlier asking for you. I had no idea what to say, so I gave him the number of your friend Betty in case she knew where you were. I hope you don't mind, but it was the only number I had. Don't worry, dear, I don't expect those reporters will hang around long if you don't want to talk to them."

Mrs. Watkins gave her younger neighbour a warm hug as she left, and Marina found Jeremy Scott's card. She called his direct line number and he answered at once.

"Hello, Marina. I didn't ring you because I thought you might be resting after all that," he began. "But when I saw the TV news, I thought we needed to talk again when you are ready. When can you come over to our offices? I want you to meet one of our senior partners who has more experience of this sort of thing. He will be here, probably until about seven. When would be a good time?"

"Well, I am a bit tired," said Marina. "And there's a crowd of reporters and TV cameras outside the flats, and I don't think I can face them. In any case, I am not supposed to talk to them, and I don't know what to say."

"Oh dear," replied Jeremy. "Look, you stay there, and we will come over to your flat. If necessary, we will say something to keep the press happy. Then it might be better if you came away with us and brought your things so that you could go somewhere quiet until this all dies down. Is there anywhere you can go?"

Marina was in a quandary. "My best friend here in Portsmouth has already had the press visiting her flat, so

I had better not go there. Let me think about it. I can't think of anyone else off-hand; I could go to my parents in London, but I don't really want to get them involved."

She began packing a few essentials into an overnight bag and decided she should try to call Betty's mobile phone number. She got an answer at once. "What's happening now?"

"It's getting a bit difficult – I am surrounded by the press here, and my lawyer has suggested I go away for a bit until things quieten down," said Marina. "I don't want to go to my folk in London while all this is going on. The press already know about your place, so that won't be any better. Any ideas where I can go?"

"Let me think," said Betty. "Look, I do have an idea. One of my friends working here at the hospital lives on a farm with her parents out in the sticks near Rowlands Castle. Let me see if she is able to help. Can I call you back?"

As soon as Marina put down her phone, it rang again. It was Jeremy to say that he and his colleague were already outside the block of flats and could she let them in. When her door buzzer rang, she heard the familiar voice of Jeremy on the intercom and this time pressed the admit button. A few minutes later, he had found his way to her door and was accompanied by a rather elegant older man in a pin-striped dark grey suit, whom he introduced as Mr. Barclay Smith.

"Come on in, Mr. Smith," said Marina. "And apologies for the muddles here, but things have been a bit hectic, as you know."

"It's Barclay-Smith, with a hyphen," he said, handing over his card. "But just call me David."

The two solicitors found seats together on the sofa, and Marina faced them in a chair, trying hard to appear relaxed as she listened to their plan.

"Judging by the TV and radio and the gang outside, this

is going to be big news for quite some time," said Barclay-Smith. "And you are going to be in the middle of it, so we would be pleased to give you any help and advice you may need. The police are involved, as you know, and the two men who interviewed you were from the security services, MI5 I think, so it's all quite a serious matter. Do you know any more about this Russian fellow beyond what you have already shared with Jeremy?"

"No, not really," said Marina. "Except all the things we chatted about on the website. He told me that he was a widower, lost his wife a couple of years ago, and was enjoying his career in the navy. He had been in a desk job and was looking for a chance to go to sea again. And then he told me he had been appointed to a ship which would visit Portsmouth. We wanted to meet when he arrived, and that's all. We spent the day together and came back here for coffee and then the police arrived and we were suddenly whisked away. It was all so sudden. He seemed such a lovely man, and he was really interested in me as well."

"Do you have any records or printouts from your computer of the messages you exchanged on line?" he asked.

"I don't think so," she said. "It may be possible to go back and recover the material on the computer, but I have never tried. And anyway, the police still have my computer."

He was interrupted by a call on Marina's phone. It was Betty.

"I've got some news," she said. "I explained your predicament to my friend Susie, and she has chatted to her parents, who say you are welcome to have their guest room for the weekend."

"Are you sure?" asked Marina. "It is a bit much to ask them to have a complete stranger to stay, especially one who is being chased by the press … and on bail from the police, for that matter."

"No, no," said Betty. "They are lovely people. I have met them a few times, and the house is quite secluded. I think they are actually a bit excited by it all. Can you get your solicitor to drive you there? Here's the address – it is Mr. and Mrs Mann, and they live at The Old Farmhouse in Dean Lane near Rowlands Castle. It's only 10 miles from here, and I will ring you back with their phone number."

"Thanks so much, Betty. It is so kind of you and your friends, and it would be really nice to get away somewhere quiet. Do I need to do anything else?"

"No – just ring them when you know what time you might arrive, and then I will go over there to see you tomorrow. Bye for now."

"That sounded promising," said David. "What's the plan?"

Marina explained the details of her conversation, and the two solicitors agreed that it sounded like a perfect solution for the time being.

Then David added, "Look here, this could all get a bit complicated, so can I ask you whether you agree to having our firm represent you in this matter? We won't send you any bills for our time at this stage, while we investigate what happens next. If it goes to court, you will probably get some sort of legal aid, or there may be other ways to cover our costs. What do you say?"

"That's kind of you," said Marina. "And it was really good to have Jeremy with me at the police station last night, so if you think you can help me deal with all this, that's fine with me. Do you know what is happening at my office? Should I talk to my boss there about my job and when I can go back?"

"Don't worry – they are in the picture, and we will keep in touch and maybe see how things are by Monday morning. So when you are ready, I suggest that you come out of the building with us to our car. I'll make a brief statement to the press, which should keep them happy for a while. You don't need to say anything – refer any questions to me. I know you are tired, but try to look strong and confident for the cameras. Is that OK?"

Marina relaxed and smiled. Then a few minutes later, she took another call from Betty with the Manns' phone number, finished packing her overnight bag and as they all left together, she locked her door behind her and tapped on the door of her neighbour. "Don't worry," she said when Mrs. Watkins answered. "These are my solicitors, and they are looking after me until this all blows over. I will be staying with friends for the weekend."

Then the three of them went down to the ground floor, and at the main entrance to the flats, they confronted the assembled group from the media. It was getting dark, and they paused on the steps with Marina in the middle while flashlight photographs were taken. Then, with the TV cameras running, David Barclay-Smith began:

"I am David Barclay-Smith, from the law firm of Henderson Partners, and together with my colleague, Jeremy Scott here, we are representing Miss Marina Peters. She has become inadvertently caught up in the matter of the Russian naval officer who has been detained by the police and MI5, and she will not be answering any questions at this stage. She will be pleased to talk to the press when she is able to do so, but at present, she would appreciate it if you did not continue to obstruct this building and inconvenience Miss Peters or her neighbours. Thank you."

There were a few shouted questions: "How long have you known the Russian?" "Is he your boyfriend?" "Where is he now?" as the solicitors escorted Marina to the car and Jeremy drove them all to their law offices in the City centre.

In David Barclay-Smith's elegantly furnished third floor

office, they began to plan the next stages. The solicitors said they would contact the CID chief, Paul Maggs, in the morning to discover when Marina could retrieve her laptop and mobile phone and to ask if and when they would need to see her again. And at that time, they would tell the police that they should now contact her through the solicitors. David also confirmed that they would stay in contact with the Commodore's office in the Dockyard and see whether Marina could have a reassuring conversation with her supervisors there.

Then Marina said she also wanted to have a longer chat with her father in the next day or two and, in particular, ask him why he had been contacted by the Russian Embassy. This revelation startled David Barclay-Smith.

"I knew from Jeremy's report that your forefathers came from Russia," he said. "But that is all history, isn't it? Why would the Embassy know about your father and why now?"

Jeremy intervened: "Perhaps there is a section at the Embassy which keeps tabs on all the Russian ex-pats in this country – just in case."

"In case of what?" asked David. "There must be thousands of them, many thousands, I would think. So they must have moved pretty quickly to have connected the news story about Aldanov with Marina's father in London already. There's more to this than meets the eye. I think Marina should talk to her father again as soon as possible and try to find out what's going on. I think she should probably tell the police about this tomorrow, and then perhaps Scotland Yard should talk to Mr. Peters."

Marina called the Manns' home number from David's office, and Mrs. Mann sounded very welcoming and understanding. She then gave driving instructions to Jeremy, who took Marina down to his car in the underground car park. They left unseen by the waiting reporters who had followed them after the doorstep interview.

It was about 10 miles from the centre of Portsmouth to the converted farmhouse, and Marina was impressed to see a couple of ponies grazing in the moonlight. Robert and Jennifer Mann heard them arriving up the long drive and were at the front door – actually, it was Rear Admiral Robert Mann, RN retired. It had been ten years since he left active service after a distinguished naval career, finally serving in the Ministry of Defence after commanding an aircraft carrier. Now he was involved mainly in charity work. David Barclay-Smith had recognised the name and address during the discussion in his office and had already phoned him in advance while Jeremy and Marina were *en route* to explain the situation in more detail. Robert said he was only too happy to "do his bit" to help and looked forward to meeting the woman concerned. He felt sure that the Navy would not have employed her if there had been any doubt about her loyalty – and "any friend of Susie's is fine with us".

The Manns gave them a warm welcome and did not ask any questions. Jeremy left to return home to Portsmouth at the end of a demanding day's work, promising to return to see Marina the next morning. Jennifer Mann gave their guest a late supper, and they all had a reassuring chat. Marina told them briefly that she was probably a police witness in the story that had been on the news and that because the press were trying to interview her, they had advised her to find somewhere to stay out of the way for the time being. The Admiral said he fully understood, and he encouraged Marina to use their telephone. Although it was now quite late, she briefly rang Betty to thank her for making the arrangement with the Mann family and for helping her to get away from the persistent press.

At last, Marina relaxed and enjoyed a long sleep in the comfort of a luxuriously furnished and equipped guest bedroom. It did not matter that she had brought only her basic toiletries and nightwear plus a change of clothes for the next day. And it was not until nearly 9 am on the Friday morning that Jennifer Mann tapped on the door with apologies for disturbing her, adding that Jeremy Scott had called to say he was on his way and would be there at about ten.

That was just about enough time for Marina to prepare for the day ahead and to enjoy a light breakfast in the sunlit kitchen overlooking the Hampshire countryside.

10.
"FIND MARINA"

On the Friday morning, the Daily Star appeared with its front-page splash and the photograph of Marina Peters – "believed to be the woman involved". The later editions of other daily papers carried more cautious stories based on the official statement. Then the weekly Portsmouth Herald was on the street and in the local newsagents, also with Marina's name and photograph displayed boldly. They also had the "exclusive" picture of the car leaving the police station, believed to be carrying the Russian. Otherwise, there was little more detail than in the Daily Star, but Gary's colourful description of the events soon had the whole town talking.

During the morning, after pressure from the media in London, another short statement was issued by the Foreign Office, releasing the names of the two people involved. It confirmed that the Russian detained in Portsmouth on Wednesday was Nikolai Aldanov, and that he had been taken to London for further questioning by the security services, and that the woman concerned was Marina Peters, a civilian employee in the Royal Navy Commodore's office in Portsmouth Dockyard. It added that she had been questioned by Portsmouth police regarding her meeting with Aldanov and released pending further inquiries.

An urgent instruction then went out from all the news editors in London to their reporters assigned to the story: "Find Marina."

There was, in fact, very little more for any of the national reporters to go on other than snippets of information from police contacts, brief conversations with one or two Dockyard workers anxious to get in on the act and a few paragraphs of background local information from Gary Andrews and Mike Morrissey – all of which only served to increase the speculation in the stories they wrote that day.

These few facts took the reporters back to Marina's home in Southsea – but all they discovered from neighbours was that she had "gone to stay with friends". But they genuinely had no idea who these friends were, or where they lived.

The Navy and the local police were saying nothing to the press either, so the reporters continued their search for any friends and colleagues who had ever known her, at her first job in London, at Holloway University and in Portsmouth. Meanwhile, in London, the press, radio and TV correspondents specialising in security matters followed up with their contacts and obtained sufficient information to confirm the involvement of MI5 in questioning the Russian. They were also able to discover through their sources that Nikolai Aldanov was now known to be an agent with the GRU in Moscow.

All this was enough to develop the story which appeared in various forms in all the media over the weekend. The Sunday papers made the most of it – and "Russian spy" was in the main headline of every report, as well as the "mystery woman".

11.
RUSSIAN CONSULAR VISIT

Little had been said during the two-hour Thursday morning drive up the A3 from Portsmouth police station back to London and to the headquarters of the MI5 counterintelligence unit by the River Thames. The Russian officer was in the back of the car, handcuffed to one of the two interrogators, repeatedly asking where they were going and demanding to talk to the Russian embassy – and getting no response from his escort.

When they arrived, the two agents handed the Russian over to a detention officer and they were there in time for the second meeting of the inter-departmental group which had been convened for the early afternoon. This just gave the officers time for a coffee and sandwich and a chance to freshen up before facing their senior management.

This time, the meeting was chaired by the MI5 Director himself – "M" no less – and he explained how the Foreign Office and Scotland Yard's National Security department were now involved and why their representatives were also around the table. Thomas Spencer began by congratulating the two agents on the success of their mission in Portsmouth to detain and question the Russian and the woman who met him from his ship. He went on to describe how during the past few weeks, a team of his investigators had been reviewing several hundred pages of correspondence between the Russian and his contact in Portsmouth, together with the photographs they had exchanged. Not only had the messages contained enough information to justify detaining the Russian for seeking to recruit a British national as an informant, but with the help of the photos taken in Portsmouth, the experts in face recognition had now identified him as an experienced officer of the GRU Russian Secret Service and not a serving Naval Lieutenant.

Then there was also the issue of whether the woman concerned had divulged confidential information, and this aspect was currently being explored in conjunction with the Ministry of Defence and Scotland Yard. Spencer added that much of this information seemed to match closely with the material the two agents had assembled from the interviews conducted in Portsmouth. A small team was assigned to prepare the legal case against Nikolai Aldanov and a timetable for proceeding with a prosecution case.

"M" confirmed that he was in agreement with the plans so far. The next step was to inform the Russian Embassy, through the official diplomatic channels of the Foreign Office, that Nikolai Aldanov was now in custody in London, pending charges relating to national security and that he would probably be formally charged in the next few days. One of M's staff left the room to pass on this instruction, and the meeting was still going on when an immediate response came from the Russian Ambassador. It declared that Aldanov had been detained illegally and demanding his immediate release and consular access to speak to him.

When the meeting was adjourned, the Home Office legal experts went into an urgent session to consider how to respond. Their meeting of minds was chaired by the head of the legal division, Henry Newbolt, and he took the group through his agenda of the issues facing them.

First, they considered the claim about detaining the Russian illegally and quickly agreed that this was a red herring which could be easily disregarded and contested if necessary. Moving on, they all agreed that they were uncomfortable with the decision to release the woman involved so early in the proceedings, particularly since the transcripts of the online conversations showed clearly that she had told Aldanov about her Russian ancestry. Had the investigators considered that she may have shared classified information in her messages? Was she really an innocent party caught up in a plan to turn her into an informant by means of a calculated romantic relationship?

Thirdly, they wanted confirmation that Miss Peters had been reminded that she had signed the Official Secrets Act and would, therefore, be careful with anyone she spoke to, particularly the press.

Finally, they returned to the decision made to release Miss Peters. Some of the legal minds were clearly uneasy about this. The chairman said that when he had asked this question earlier, he had been told that MI5 regarded Aldanov as the real target of their investigations and that Miss Peters' most important role now would be as a witness in a future trial of the Russian spy.

Henry Newbolt closed the meeting and said he would report the legal concerns to the MI5 Director; and he would continue to provide further advice as needed. With all this in mind, he went on to a meeting with the Director to review the options. They agreed that they could not deny Aldanov the opportunity for a consular visit from an official from the Russian Embassy and an interpreter if necessary. Then he would be formally charged with offences under national security regulations and be remanded in custody while the case against him was prepared.

Meanwhile, the Director made it clear that he supported

the decision regarding the release of Miss Peters because they intended to "throw the book" at the Russian agent, who was a valuable asset in the hands of MI5 and MI6. She was their key witness, and they needed her input. They also needed as much time as possible to investigate and grill the Russian.

The decision to allow consular access to Aldanov was transmitted to the Russian embassy via the Foreign Office, and within a few minutes, a reply was received asking for a location and a time for the meeting, preferably within the next two hours.

The wheels turned quickly, and just an hour later, a car arrived at the entrance to the MI5 Thameside building, and the two passengers strode inside to the security checking zone. Their credentials were checked, and they were identified as a member of the Russian diplomatic staff and an interpreter. They were expected, of course, and so an officer was waiting in the lobby area to greet them. He took them swiftly by lift to a basement room where Nikolai Aldanov was brought in, without handcuffs, for an initial unsupervised meeting. "You have 15 minutes," they were told.

They were all too aware that their discussion would be monitored, no doubt by a Russian-speaking officer in the department, so they were cautious and circumspect, mainly confirming Aldanov's identity and asking him to describe the circumstances of his detention and whether he had been mistreated in any way. His replies did not reveal anything new to those listening in; he insisted that he was a Russian Navy officer and wanted to resume his duties on his ship as soon as possible and asked for the Embassy's help. Those listening noted that he did not mention his intended meeting with his contact in the Dockyard, and neither was this mentioned by the Russian interviewing him.

After the assigned 15 minutes, a senior MI5 officer

re-entered the room, together with Thomas Spencer, and the Russian diplomat immediately stood up and proclaimed, "Lieutenant Aldanov is a serving officer of the Russian Navy, and we demand his immediate release and your apologies for the way he has been treated since his ship arrived in the UK. Also, it was contrary to international law for your officers to detain him and to then hold him in custody without stating the offence which he is alleged to have committed."

Spencer replied, slowly and carefully through the interpreter, "Your questions have been noted, gentlemen, but this is a matter of national security, and we have reason to believe that Mr. Aldanov was not a serving naval officer as you stated, but is in fact an official with the GRU and that he engaged in activities which may endanger the security of this country. We intend to pursue this matter further, and he will remain in custody until we are ready to proceed with an appropriate charge. Your embassy will be informed through the usual channels, and we have nothing further to say at this time. Good afternoon, gentlemen."

At this point, the two MI5 officers marched swiftly out of the room, and the custody officer, who had been waiting at the door, led a protesting Aldanov away to the secure holding cells nearby. The Russian diplomats tried to respond, but their protests were ignored and they were escorted from the building to their waiting car for the short drive back to the embassy in Kensington Palace Gardens.

There they reported on the meeting to their Ambassador and then prepared a full outline of the situation in a lengthy, strictly confidential message to the head of GRU in Moscow. After describing the position so far, it went on to set out the reasons why they believed that Aldanov had been careless in the execution of his mission and that, as a consequence, his cover as a serving naval officer had been blown.

There was nothing further they could do at this stage other than wait to see what action the British might take. Also, in a footnote to the message, they asked why the London bureau of GRU had not been informed in advance about Aldanov's mission to the UK.

A swift response came back on the protected and confidential message line: "What do you know about the woman involved? Is she a crucial party in this matter? Please consider ways to contact her and discover whether she will corroborate the story that this was simply the start of a romantic relationship. Also explore a way to discover more about her family connections with Russia."

The GRU's assistant head of station at the London Embassy, who had posed as the interpreter at the meeting at MI5 headquarters, warmed to this idea and replied to Moscow that he would work on it. He went away to discuss the options with his team and began to prepare a plan. It started with a decision to send two of his most experienced agents, a man and a woman, to Portsmouth posing as tourists to explore the situation and with the aim of making contact with Marina Peters.

12.
IGOR AND SVETLANA

It was not only the press and broadcasting reporters who were trying to locate Marina Peters in Portsmouth. On the Thursday evening, the Russian couple despatched from the Embassy arrived in Portsmouth by train, with minimal luggage, and used the GPS map on their iPhone to find their way to Marina's address in Southsea. It was a long walk, nearly 30 minutes, but it helped them to find their bearings in the city. Nearby, they spotted a large seafront house offering B&B Vacancies – not surprising since it was now October – and the proprietor welcomed them with open arms. Igor and Svetlana said they wanted to stay through the weekend, and she took them up to her best room at £100 per night – including breakfast between 8 and 9 am.

They quickly checked the wi-fi signal and then agreed to take the room, with twin beds and *en suite* bathroom – just what they wanted as their base for the next few days. They signed in as Mr. and Mrs. Ericsen from Sweden.

After settling in, they went out into the cool evening sea-breeze and began their reconnaissance of the area on their way to find a meal. They soon discovered a pizza restaurant and during their meal, they prepared a plan. This began by returning to a busy pub they had passed an hour earlier, where they soon merged with the crowd as they ordered a pint of best bitter and a cider.

"Where are you from?" asked the barman. They replied, in their heavily accented English, "From Sweden, and this is our first visit in this country outside of London. What goes on here?"

The group around them at the bar were intrigued by some new faces out of season and more interestingly, from overseas. They soon made them welcome, and between them, they provided a good briefing on places to see – including *HMS Victory* and the *Mary Rose*. This led to conversation about the Dockyard, and one of the locals interrupted and said, "Hey, have you seen the news this evening? It's all been on the telly about a Russian spy in the Dockyard…"

The two visitors tried not to look too interested, but they encouraged the man to tell them more.

"Yeh. It's all happening here," he continued. "There's a Russian ship arrived here, and a guy came ashore and was arrested by some spooks from MI5. And there's a local girl involved, too – it was all on the TV news."

Another man in the group chimed in. "They say the girl lives around here. She works for the Navy in the Dockyard and was arrested at the same time. So, she's probably caught up in the spy thing as well."

And a third added to the discussion. "I think I know her. A pal of mine told me about her earlier this evening. He lives in the same block of flats, and he says he thinks I met her there once. A good-looker too – reckon she's one of those Bond girls, then?"

"Get your pal to bring her in for a drink, then," said the first man.

The beer was doing the talking, and the group went on exchanging spy stories. Soon, the two visiting Russians had absorbed enough local gossip and they slipped away and walked back to their B&B to consider their next moves.

Next morning, after a full English breakfast, their first objective was to pay a visit to Marina's flat. On the way, they passed a newsagent and found the Daily Star with its front-page story and picture, which surprised them with so much information. But it seemed to confirm the information they had heard in the pub. They were concerned that the man from the pub might recognise them if they went together to the block of flats, so Svetlana put a long dark wig over her short hairstyle, found a pair of spectacles and walked alone to the entrance which they had identified the previous evening. She tried to ignore the small group of reporters waiting by the front entrance and pressed the bell with the name of Miss Peters.

"I don't think she's there," said one of the reporters. "We are waiting in case she comes back this morning. Who are you with?"

"Nothing to do with you," replied Svetlana fiercely. "I am here on a business matter."

This got the reporters' attention, and they tried to get into conversation. "What business?" "Do you know Marina?" "Any idea where she might be?" But Svetlana ignored them, and when she got no response from repeated calls on the bell-push, she walked away and was joined by Igor who had been watching from a distance.

"What now?" they asked each other. The answer came when they saw a police car pull up at the flats and a uniformed officer went to the door carrying a brown cardboard box. He ignored questions from the press group but also got no reply from the entry system and went back to his parked car. Igor gave him a wave and walked up to the car; the officer wound down the car window. "Are you looking for Marina Peters?" Igor asked.

"Who wants to know?" said the young policeman.

"I'm a relative from London," said Igor. "And I was very concerned that she might be involved in this Russian business on the news. I want to see if she is all right. Any idea where I can find her?"

"No – sorry," came the reply. "The only other contact I have is her solicitor here in Portsmouth. He's with Henderson Partners in mid-town, a Mr. Scott, I think." He closed the car window and drove off, taking the box with him.

The two Russians quickly located the address for Henderson Partners on their iPhone, hailed a taxi, and followed the trail. At a modern city-centre office block, they saw that the law firm had offices on the first two floors, and the reception desk was manned. They were there in time to see the same police car driving away, and they went in together and asked for Mr. Scott. The receptionist asked the reason for their inquiry, and they volunteered that it was in connection with his client, Miss Marina Peters.

"He is not here at the moment" she replied. "But I was about to ring him anyway because I have just had this box delivered for Miss Peters by the police. Can I say who wants him?"

"We are her relatives from London, and we want to find out if she is all right," Igor replied.

The receptionist dialled a number and then spoke. "Jeremy? Yes, it's Sue at the office. It's a bit busy here. The police have just delivered a big box for you which they said contains Miss Peters' computer and mobile phone. I signed for it on your behalf. We've had the press here looking for you. And now a couple of her relatives have arrived from London, inquiring about her. What shall I tell them?

And turning to Igor and Svetlana, she said, "He says are you her parents?"

"Tell him no, but we are relations and would just like to see her, if possible," said Igor.

The receptionist had a further conversation, then rang off and said, "Mr. Scott says he will be back in the office later and could you come here again at about 2 pm? He will talk to you then."

They went away to a nearby coffee shop and ordered two Americanos. They were about to discuss their options when Igor's mobile phone rang; it was their boss at the Embassy with some important new information. Some phone calls had been monitored that indicated that the woman was no longer in Portsmouth. They said they were working on discovering her new location and the two agents should stand by for new instructions.

13.
THE FARMHOUSE

While she was waiting for Jeremy Scott to arrive at the farmhouse on Friday morning, Marina called her father again. Victor Peters was relieved to hear from his daughter and to know that she was comfortably housed by friends for the weekend. He had now seen the news from Portsmouth on TV and in the morning paper and wanted to visit her as soon as possible; he said he was still perplexed by his call from the Russian Embassy in which they had asked to meet him to talk about his daughter's involvement with the Lieutenant from the *Admiral Essen*. He was not sure what to do next but said he would return the Embassy's call and then get in touch with Marina again. She said she had not yet seen the morning paper because she was "out in the countryside" and would probably get it later, but she was horrified when he said her picture was on the front page.

She told him where she was staying and gave him the phone number, adding, "Don't tell anyone where I am and don't ring my mobile – the police still have my phone."

When Jeremy arrived, they settled in the sitting room with cups of coffee, and Marina told him about her conversations with her father. They were interrupted when Jeremy Scott took the phone call from the receptionist at his office with the news about the box returned by the police and the visit by two Russians claiming to be Marina's relatives. Marina said she had no idea who they might be, so Jeremy decided that he would go back to the office in the city at lunchtime and be there to meet up with them in the early afternoon.

After hearing about this further complication, Jeremy decided to hook up with David Barclay-Smith, who was still at his home in Old Portsmouth. On a three-way call, they began by discussing why the Russian Embassy had contacted Victor Peters. So far as Marina knew, he had never had any reason to be in touch with the Embassy – although, of course, it was only natural that he had a network of friends in London with Russian ancestry, and she knew they met from time to time. But they had been business people, not diplomats, she insisted.

"Let's review this," said David. "The Russian Embassy's intelligence people are told by the Foreign Office that the naval officer Aldanov has been detained for questioning by MI5. They also learn that the investigation is about his contact with Marina, who works in an important Royal Navy section. They know from the exchange of messages recorded in Moscow that Marina's family came from Russia back in the 1930s and had changed their name from Petrov to Peters. They also knew that Aldanov's mission was to find a way to recruit Marina as an informant, possibly through a romantic relationship."

Marina looked horrified by this and David went on: "Sorry Marina, but that's how it looks. The Russians have now sent two of their spooks to Portsmouth to try to find you. So now, what are their options? They will discover that you were released by the police after being interviewed, presumably because MI5 believed that you had become innocently involved with your online friend. No doubt they will need you to testify against Aldanov. So why are the Russian Embassy chasing your father? Do they want to use your father to persuade you to deny that there was any suggestion of passing confidential information?"

Marina interrupted. "They don't need to involve my father about that."

"Well," continued David. "Do they think that, in the long run, you and possibly your father could be useful to them? Could they have some information they could use to put pressure on your father and maybe use it to exploit your experience and knowledge about the Navy? Aldanov at least succeeded in discovering your potential value through his subterfuge. I think you should have another word with your father, so I suggest you call him now – and ask Jeremy to call me again afterwards."

They cleared the phone line, and Marina went to find Mrs. Mann and asked if she could use their phone again. Admiral Mann had gone out to his golf club for the day, anyway, and the house was quiet, she said, so go ahead.

Victor answered the phone and said, "I'm glad you rang. The man at the Embassy has just called me again and asked if he could drive me to Portsmouth to meet up with you. I said you were not at your flat and I had no idea where you were. I don't know who he is, and I expect he will call again. What do you think?"

"I'd rather just see you, Dad, so that we can have a quiet chat about all this. Hold on a moment, I have a very helpful solicitor here with me, and I will see what he thinks."

Marina then gave this information to Jeremy, who also thought that if her father wanted to meet up, they should just go ahead, and there was no reason why he should involve the Russian Embassy man. Marina relayed this view to her father, who said he would go ahead and get a train to Portsmouth as soon as possible and let her know when he arrived, hopefully later that afternoon. She gave him the Mann's phone number again and ended the call.

On the way back to Portsmouth in his car, Jeremy called his boss at home again and told him about the latest developments.

"This is sounding a bit sinister," said David. "Three Russians now want to meet Marina, and they are up to no good, and one of them is talking to her father. I think I will let the police know about this. I'll get back to you"

David called the Portsmouth CID and told them that he was now advising Marina Peters; he was eventually put through to Detective Superintendent Maggs.

"You may know some of this already," he began, "but there are a few things going on I thought I should share with you. First of all, Miss Peters wanted to get away from the press gathered at her front door, and through a friend, she has gone away for the weekend to a house in the country near Rowlands Castle. As you probably saw on TV, we escorted her out of her flat, and my colleague, Jeremy Scott, then drove her to stay with these friends, who turn out to be Rear Admiral Robert Mann and his wife. That was a surprise, I must say, but the young lady obviously has some well-connected friends. Anyway, Jeremy went back to visit her this morning, and two things have happened. First, Marina rang her father to reassure him and to let her parents know where she was staying. He then told her that the Russian Embassy people have been in touch with him again today, offering to take him to Portsmouth to see his daughter."

Superintendent Maggs interrupted. "If the Embassy is in contact with Victor Peters, they will also have traced the call he had from Marina, so they probably know where she is by now. What did she tell him to do?"

"On Jeremy's advice, she told him to ignore the call from the Embassy and just get on a train to Portsmouth and let her know when he arrived. But that's not all," continued

David. "Two foreigners – a man and a woman – arrived at my office this morning and told the receptionist that they were relatives of Marina and wanted to see her. From their accents, we think they may have been Russians. There was no one else at the office who could help, so she rang Jeremy, and he told her he would meet them there at about two this afternoon. And by the way, Marina does not know of any Russian relatives in London who might be here and wanting to see her."

"Well, that's all very interesting… thank you for this," said Maggs. "So there are now three Russians who want to see Marina, and we still have to follow up our inquiries with her and with the navy people. The plot thickens. I imagine they knew about your firm's connection in this from your interview outside the flats last night. You know, I think I'll get a couple of my people to go to your offices this afternoon to take a look at the Russian couple when they arrive and maybe discover who they really are."

Maggs next reached his contact at MI5, Tom Spencer, on a secure line and briefed him on these latest developments in Portsmouth. "OK," he was told. "Sounds like a couple of agents from the London section of GRU are sniffing around. I doubt if you will discover much by meeting them, but it will be good to let them know you are aware of their activities. Can you get someone to snatch a picture of them so that we can check them out? And by the way, the most important thing you can do is to keep the woman under wraps. Bring her in for more questioning if necessary. In any case, we will need to talk to her again on Monday."

The two most experienced detectives on duty in Portsmouth CID were then briefed by DS Maggs, and they set off to keep a discreet watch on the offices of Henderson Partners, ready to confront the Russian visitors.

14.
VICTOR PETERS ARRIVES

Soon after Jeremy had driven off on Friday morning to return to his office, Susie Mann arrived at her parents' house, together with Betty McGuire. They had both arranged a day off at the hospital, and Marina was relieved to see them; she could hardly stop hugging and thanking Betty for all her help. They all had much to chat about over a girlie lunch, and Susie and her mother became increasingly apprehensive as the story of Marina's Russian contact emerged. They began to worry about what they had unwittingly become involved in.

When Admiral Mann returned during the afternoon, his wife quickly followed him to their bedroom, where he planned to quietly change his clothes and take a rest. He was immediately faced by a rather tense Jennifer. "Do you know that this Marina is not just a friend of Betty's, but she is apparently caught up in this Russian spy business at the Dockyard? She's here to avoid the press, and there are also a couple of Russians in Portsmouth looking for her, too. I can sense that it's all going to get messy. Do we have to get involved?"

"Don't worry, m'dear," replied Robert Mann, calmly. "I've already had a briefing from her lawyer in Portsmouth, who is a good egg. I also plan to chat to the Commodore she works for. If any reporters or Russians think they can find her here, I will deal with them. So relax and let the poor girl recover from a very trying couple of days. Let's find a cup of tea."

The Admiral took his tea into the sitting room and joined the ladies. He wanted to know more about Marina and quietly questioned her about her background and her job at the Dockyard. She then began to tell him about her online relationship with the Russian Lieutenant until she was interrupted by Mrs. Mann bringing the cordless phone. "Your father is on the line."

Marina discovered that he had just arrived at Portsmouth railway station.

"Are you alone?" she asked. He said he was, and she asked him to hold on while she chatted with her friends. Admiral Mann quickly took the initiative.

"Tell him I will drive into Portsmouth to meet him, and you had better come with me to be sure we find the right man. Tell him to go into the station café and wait there – we'll be there in about half an hour."

A few minutes later, Marina and Betty were both in the Admiral's large Mercedes car and heading to Portsmouth, discussing where might be the best place to have a discreet meeting. They suspected that the press might still be keeping a watch on Marina's flat and possibly Betty's too. Using Betty's mobile phone, they hooked up with Jeremy Scott, now back in his office, who then connected them all with David Barclay-Smith. They eliminated various options for a meeting, including the law firm's offices, which Jeremy said had just been visited again by the two Russian agents. After considering a couple of local hotels, David said, "Look, just bring them down to my house. I think Robert knows where I live in Old Portsmouth."

At the railway station, Marina and Betty went in to find

the café and Victor Peters while Robert Mann waited in the car. It was very busy, but they soon found him, looking around anxiously with just a cup of coffee and a newspaper at a discreet corner table. Marina gave her father a warm hug and said they needed to go straight away. In the car, she introduced him to Betty and to Admiral Mann and explained that they were going to a lawyer's house, where they could have a long quiet chat. It was just five minutes to Old Portsmouth and to the Barclay-Smith's elegant 18th-century home overlooking the Solent and the Isle of Wight. David was at the window and saw them drive up and park. He came to the front door and welcomed them – "Very good to see you again, David," said the Admiral as they went up a flight of stairs to the sitting room with a sea view. It was the view Marina had enjoyed just two days earlier as she'd waited for the Russian ships to arrive; it seemed like a week ago.

David quickly explained that Marina needed to have a quiet chat with her father, and he then took Robert and Betty into his adjoining study so that Marina and her father could be alone for a while.

Robert offered them a scotch, but David said "Thanks, but maybe later" and took the opportunity to call Jeremy to discover what had happened at the office that afternoon.

"Well, I didn't get the opportunity to talk to them," explained Jeremy. "They were intercepted at the door by two men who turned out to be CID officers, and after a short chat, the couple disappeared, and the police officers came into the office and said not to worry because we wouldn't be hearing from them again. And that was it."

"OK," said David. "At the moment I have Marina and her father here at my home, and they are catching up with each other as we speak. Admiral Mann brought them down here, and I am not sure what happens next. You go off and enjoy the weekend, and we will regroup at the office on Monday morning."

"By the way, David, I still have the box here for Marina – it's her laptop computer and mobile phone returned this morning by the police."

"I don't think we should hold on to it," said David. "Can you drop it in to me on your way home and give it back to her?"

David then called Portsmouth CID again and was immediately put through to Detective Superintendent Maggs who told him that the matter had become more complicated since they last spoke. His officers had confronted the two Russians as planned. They had given their names and addresses as "care of the Russian Embassy" in London but had refused to say why they were in Portsmouth or why they had been calling at the solicitor's office. They had managed to snatch photos of the couple approaching the office, and they had now been positively identified by Scotland Yard as known GRU agents based in London.

"Now, this is the latest," continued DS Maggs. "MI5 has insisted that we keep the girl Marina under wraps. They think the Russians probably know the farmhouse address by now, so MI5 say that we should drive her to London as soon as possible and they will take care of her there for the time being. So it will be out of our hands."

David then told Maggs two things that were surprises for him. Firstly, that Marina and her friend Betty were now at his house in Old Portsmouth, and secondly, that Marina's father had arrived by train from London and was now with her. And he explained that Admiral Mann had brought them into town from his house near Rowlands Castle.

"At the moment, Mr. Peters is telling his daughter about the contacts he has had from someone at the Russian Embassy asking to meet with Marina. I will catch up with them both in a few minutes. So as things stand," continued David, "Mr. Peters will be on the late evening train back to London, and Marina is going back to the Manns' house in the country until we know what happens next."

Maggs thought quickly and said, "This is getting serious. In these circumstances, I think MI5 will probably want us to take father and daughter to Thameside in London together as soon as possible, and then they can decide what to do next. So hold on and I'll call you back."

15.
A MAN NAMED JACK

Marina and her father were both tense as they sat together in the Mann's sitting room with their tray of tea and biscuits, brought to them stylishly by the lady of the house. Neither knew quite where to start the conversation, and the initial small talk while the tea was poured by Mrs. Mann did not last very long.

As soon as she left the room, Victor Peters asked: "What are you involved in, Marina?" And he did not really believe her when she tried to explain her the online meeting with the Russian and his arrival on the ship in Portsmouth a couple of days earlier. He knew his daughter well enough to realise that she was not telling him the whole story. As they skirted around the matter, she, in turn, began to suspect, for the first time, that there was something more to her father's contact with the Russian Embassy.

"This is not just a budding romance then, is it?" he asked.

"I had never actually spoken to the man before he arrived here," she replied insistently. "And then we were picked up by the police just a few hours later after I had shown him around Portsmouth. I haven't seen him since. What did the Russian embassy say to you?"

"They asked me if I had seen the newspaper story and whether I had talked to you about it."

"So how did they know where to find you? The paper did not mention you at all."

"Well, I expect I am on their records somewhere because of our Russian connections. The man who called said his name was Jack and he just wanted to talk to me about what they had read and then he offered to drive me to Portsmouth to see you."

"Why would you be on their records, Dad? You've never had any reason to be in touch with them over the years, have you?"

"No, of course not," he replied – rather unconvincingly, Marina thought, just as David and Admiral Mann came into the room.

"Sorry to interrupt, but there seems to have been a change of plans," said David. "The Russian Embassy people are very anxious to talk to you, Marina, and they have even sent a couple of their spooks to Portsmouth today to find you. The press are still looking for you, as well, and the local police say this is now out of their hands and that the MI5 people in London are calling the shots. They want to keep you both under wraps for the time being and I understand that the police are now arranging cars to drive you both back to London, maybe even later this evening, and they will then look after you both. I am waiting for another call with more details."

Marina and her father looked at each other, saying nothing for a while. Then Mr. Peters suddenly broke the silence. "But I've got a return train ticket," he protested.

"That's being silly, Dad," said Marina. "This all sounds a bit more serious than I thought… I think we really have no alternative but to go along with it."

"That would be my advice, too," said David. "But remember that we are here to help you and we also have good contacts with lawyers in London who can be briefed to meet you there if you need them."

Admiral Mann looked bewildered by all that he had just heard and asked how he could help. The answer was "not much, but thanks anyway." And a few minutes later, Jeremy arrived with the much-travelled cardboard box, and Marina was reunited at last with her laptop and her mobile phone – but was unsure what to do with them. Also, if she was going to London, she said she would need to collect some further belongings from her Southsea flat.

When DS Maggs called David again, he had more information about the logistics. It had now been decided to send the two police cars to London at about 8 pm – one would pick up Mr. Peters and take him back to his home, and the other would take Marina, with an escort, direct to MI5 HQ. He added that they were also finding her a room in London for the night.

The two police cars created a little interest for the neighbours as they arrived at the Barclay-Smith home in Old Portsmouth. But there was not much to see as they quickly loaded their respective passengers after Marina and her father had exchanged a parting hug – but no further words. They all thanked the Admiral Mann rather hurriedly for all his help and Marina also had a hug for a somewhat bewildered Betty. David was as positive as ever and reassured the group that everything would be fine. Jeremy offered to drive Betty back to her home, just a mile away – and within a couple of minutes, all the cars had driven away and a quiet evening descended on Old Portsmouth again.

It had been agreed that Marina's driver and the accompanying escort would stop first at her flat in Southsea and that together they would be able to safely ignore any press or even Russians who might still be hanging around. When they arrived at the flat, all was quiet apart from one reporter sitting in his car outside. He watched a police officer follow Marina into the block with her overnight bag and her cardboard box. Once inside, she put her laptop back on her desk and the mobile phone in her handbag, pleased to be reunited with it again. Then she quickly packed a small wheelie suitcase with some additional clothes and toiletries, locked her door and then knocked on her neighbour's door to say she would be gone for a few days. They were soon speeding up the A3 to London, quickly losing the one press car which tried to follow.

16.
THE "SAFE" FLAT

As the first of the two police cars sped up the A3 and M3 towards London, Victor Peters called his wife Shona to reassure her that all was well and that he was returning by car. He gave her an approximate time of arrival, and as she watched for the car, she was alarmed to see him being dropped off by the police. She wanted to know the whole story, but firstly told him: "Before I forget, that Russian fellow from the embassy rang again, and he wants you to call him back as soon as possible."

Victor told her that the Russian could wait, and over a late supper, he described his day – or as much of it as he thought necessary. Shona had already seen most of the details in the newspaper and on the TV news, and the most important thing for her was to know that Marina's part in the story was entirely innocent. Victor explained that she was being kept away from the press until she was able to give evidence against the Russian spy. He told his wife that Marina had also travelled to London separately that evening in another police car and was being looked after safely.

"That Russian must have taken advantage of her friendly nature," said Shona after thinking about the situation. "But it was a bit careless of her to get involved with him, anyway. There must be lots of nice men out there looking for friendship without getting mixed up in all this. Do you think she knew she was taking a chance?"

"Well," said her father, sadly, "I think it was the Russian thing that got her interest – you know, my family links and all that, which are quite important to her. But she's a big girl now, making her way in the world, doing an important job and looking after herself. Now, what number do I ring to speak to that Russian?"

It was a mobile number, written by Shona on the message pad, so Victor went to his desk in the study and made the call, which was answered immediately

"Sorry to call you so late," he began. "This is Victor Peters. I understand you have been in touch again, and I thought it might be urgent."

"Yes, where are you?" came the reply.

"At home. Why are you calling me?"

"We have been reading about your daughter Marina in the newspapers and I thought we had better have a chat. Do you know where she is? We would very much like to contact her."

"No, not really. I have been to Portsmouth today to see her. She's fine but just a bit involved in this incident with one of your navy people. What's your name, and can I call you again on this number if I get any further news?"

"Just call me Jack. I am at the Russian embassy, and I think we should meet up as soon as possible. When can we get together?"

"Leave it with me – I'll call you again in a day or two." Victor hung up and told his wife, "I just spoke to that Russian who rang earlier. He is at the embassy and taking an interest in this business about the Russian officer and Marina, and he wants to meet me for a chat. I think it will wait until after the weekend. I'm very tired. Let's get some sleep."

Meanwhile, Marina had arrived at the MI5 headquarters by the Thames, where she was met in the entrance lobby by a female officer who introduced herself as Patricia and said she would be taking care of her for a few days.

"We have some comfortable digs for you just around the corner," she said, picking up Marina's bags and setting off along the road and then turning right into a modern apartment block. They took the lift to the eighth floor and found number 83, which turned out to be a quite luxurious two-bedroomed apartment with a view out across the river and the lights of London at night.

Patricia was about the same age as Marina and dressed in casual jeans and jacket. She was warm and friendly as she took Marina into one of the bedrooms and showed her all the facilities of the flat, including a kitchen with a well-stocked refrigerator and freezer.

"This is where I stay when work keeps me here late at night. I will be in the other bedroom tonight, and we each have our own bathrooms, so we should be okay," she explained. "As it's quite late, why don't you get what you need to eat from the fridge, and we'll call it a night. We can have a chat over breakfast at about 8.30? Sleep well."

Marina made a cheese sandwich, sat on her bed and collected her thoughts. She felt her whole being had suddenly been taken over by the police, the press and the events of the last 48 hours. But at least she was safe and comfortable for the night, and maybe she would discover more in the morning. She prepared herself a hot drink, went quickly to bed and slept soundly.

17.
ALDANOV IN COURT

The news story remained in the headlines over the weekend. The reports were mostly speculation about Russian spying activities, with Marina as the "mystery woman". A few more "facts" had been obtained from neighbours and co-workers in the Dockyard. However, Marina's whereabouts remained unknown until early on the Sunday morning, when there was another tip-off. Mike Morrissey was reading the results of his handiwork in the Sunday papers when his police CID contact who rang him again.

"You're probably still working on the Russian officer story," he said. "Well, when I came in this morning, I heard that we sent two cars off on Friday evening to drive to MI5 in London, and one of them was supposed to be picking up the woman in the case, Marina Peters. That's all I know at the moment, but I'll let you know if I hear any more."

An appreciative Mike was quickly in action and he drove to the Southsea flat again, and on getting no response from Marina's number, he tried the neighbour he had spoken to a couple of days earlier. "Yes, she popped in last night to say she would be away for a few days," he was told by Mrs. Watkins. "She had a suitcase, and when I looked out, I am sure I saw a police car outside."

That was all that Mike needed by way of confirmation,

and he was able to prepare a new story for the Monday papers to say that Marina Peters was now being questioned by MI5 in London about her rendezvous with the Russian Lieutenant. The news editors in London tried to check this news, but no further statements were forthcoming from Scotland Yard, the Home Office or the Foreign Office during the day. This did not stop further speculation as the new story evolved into a major security inquiry. In Monday's papers, it was illustrated with front-page pictures and there was TV coverage of the three Russian frigates leaving Portsmouth Harbour – but without Lieutenant Aldanov on board. It was speculated by the press that he and Marina would shortly appear in court on charges relating to the information exchanged between them in their online conversations..

Meanwhile, MI5 officers continued to question Aldanov through Sunday, with an attaché from the Russian embassy present, and by the end of the day, he was charged with a breach of national security by attempting to obtain confidential information from a civilian working for the Royal Navy. He appeared briefly at the Westminster Magistrate's Court on Monday morning and was remanded to a high-security prison pending trial.

After the hearing, there was another statement from the Foreign Office:

"Further to the statement issued on Friday, investigations carried out by the security services have confirmed that Nikolai Aldanov, who was detained in Portsmouth last week, is an experienced agent employed by the Russian secret service known as the GRU. After questioning by MI5, he appeared in court in London today charged with offences relating to national security, and he was remanded in custody to stand trial on a date to

be arranged. The Russian embassy is being kept fully informed. The British woman who was detained at the same time is helping MI5 with their enquiries but has not been charged at this stage."

Meanwhile, Tom Spencer and his investigative team at MI5, together with an MI6 representative, met again early on Monday morning. They began by reconsidering their view of Marina's involvement with Aldanov by discussing a new, detailed analysis of the 100-plus page transcript of their online exchanges. Also, they now had to consider the possible role of her father. They now knew that he had maintained his contacts with other Russian emigres in London and that he was obviously known to the Russian embassy, who had been trying to make contact with him since the story appeared about his daughter. They recognised that following his return from Portsmouth on Friday evening, it was likely that Russian agents had, in fact, already made contact, and it was quickly decided to place him under surveillance. But they would not yet try to formally interview him as part of the current operation.

The meeting went on for more than an hour and ranged over various possibilities. Were either Victor Peters or Marina already operating as Russian informants? It was agreed that a joint evidence-gathering operation should begin at once. They also began to speculate whether there was now an opportunity for either of the Peters to become MI5 informants – or even double agents? Or if they were not willing to risk their British citizenship in that way, did their Russian contacts provide a basis to develop their value as MI6 operatives? It was also noted that among Marina's exchanges with Aldanov, she had said she was eager to visit her ancestral roots in Russia. How could this be exploited?

As these creative ideas were explored, Spencer was pensive

for a few moments and then said, "How do you think Moscow sees this? Their guy goes fishing and comes up with an online date with an English girl who just happens to be working inside the Royal Navy comms office – and also just happens to have Russian ancestry. Was that a lucky coincidence? They probably got their London station to investigate the woman and discovered that her family was already in their records, or at least her father was. I wonder why? Did they know she was working in a sensitive section of the British navy in Portsmouth? They certainly went to all the trouble of getting their man on an operational navy ship as a Lieutenant which could be routed via Portsmouth to drop him off and meet his contact. There's obviously much more in this than we know at the moment. For example, they knew that all the exchanges between the couple were on an open website, so they must have guessed that we knew all about his arrival and would probably follow him. Let's all go away and think about all this some more …."

He then paused and, as an aside, added, "You know, this Marina is a rather interesting lady – smart, intelligent and with a Russian interest. She could be a useful asset to us."

In conclusion, Spencer emphasised to the meeting that they must also not lose sight of their primary objective – now that they held Aldanov, they needed to build a strong case against him and secure a conviction, based on Marina Peters' testimony. Members of the team were given their assignments, and the next stage was for MI5 interrogators to further question Marina as a potential key witness, but at the same time to weigh up these further questions and longer-term possibilities.

18.
AN MI5 RECRUIT?

Marina's "minder", Patricia, was assigned to ensure that they had a quiet weekend, and although they could not resist getting the Sunday papers when they walked out along the Embankment in the morning, they avoided talking too much about the Russian situation. They had lunch at a riverside restaurant and chatted about their careers to date, their families and their boyfriends. Later on, they ordered pizzas to be delivered in the evening while they watched TV.

On Monday morning, the instruction was for Patricia to take Marina to a meeting in the office soon after 10 am – where she found herself in an interview room, confronted by two MI5 officials. One was a specialist interrogator who introduced himself as Tony, and the other was Tom Spencer, who said he was the senior officer coordinating the inquiry into her relationship with Nikolai Aldanov.

Tony began by explaining that she was not facing any charges but was obviously a key witness in any action which might follow involving Aldanov. In front of him, he had the 100-plus pages of transcripts from their online exchanges, which, he said, had been carefully analysed.

"Did you feel you were being encouraged to share information about your job with him?" he asked.

"Well, not at the time," she replied. "We both asked questions about each other's lives, just to get to know each other, I suppose."

"Do you know now that he was duping you into believing that he was a naval officer in Sevastopol when he was really an intelligence officer in Moscow chatting to you from inside Russia's secret service headquarters?"

"Oh, no! Are you serious? I am sure you are, of course, but gosh, this is really a shock to me. I suppose I first began to realise that something was not right about it all from things your people said to me in Portsmouth – but not this. Is he really a spy, then?"

"We'll find out. Do you remember him asking you about the new Queen Elizabeth aircraft carrier?"

"Well yes, of course. It had just arrived in Portsmouth when we were in touch, and I could see it from my office – but it was not a secret. All the newspapers had pictures of it – it was enormous and dwarfed everything else around it. We were all talking about it."

"Did he want to know any more information about the ship? When it would become operational, for example?"

"I don't really remember now, but I didn't know very much, anyway. He was obviously interested, and I might have mentioned it again when it sailed off to go on exercises and then visited New York – but that was all in the papers, as well. If you have the transcripts there you probably know more than I can recall."

"It is pretty clear to me that he was probing for information – in fact, this sort of thing came up quite often."

"I don't remember thinking that at the time – we just wrote chatty notes to each other like any other couple might do, and obviously we had the navy and ships as a common interest. But I don't have any confidential information in my job."

"Did you wonder why you had to sign the Official Secrets Act, then?"

"It just seemed like something routine to me, but I am sure I was careful."

Tony shuffled through his file and then asked, "Did you mention that some other British ships were operating in the Med when he told you he would be heading that way?"

"If I did, it was just to show him that I was interested in where he was going. I think we talked about Malta, but I am sure he mentioned the Med first. I know where all our ships are when they are at sea, but I certainly didn't tell him anything confidential that I can remember."

"That may well be the case," said Tony sternly. "But it looks as though he was softening you up and that he thought he was on to a valuable source of information in the long run."

"Yes, I think I can see that now – but he seemed such an interesting and friendly sort of man, and I was really interested in meeting a Russian. I have always wanted to start finding out more about where my family came from, and I suppose that was the main thing on my mind when I was asking him questions about himself."

The interrogator then continued by reading extracts from the online exchanges and pointing out the extracts which had been of concern to the security services.

"This was a potentially dangerous liaison between the Russian GRU and the Royal Navy because you were clearly close to the heart of naval operations. We have been analysing all the things you said, and it is probably true that you did not pass on anything specifically confidential, but we can see where he was leading you."

"I realise that now," said a rather cowed Marina. "I am really sorry. What happens now?"

At this point, Tom Spencer stepped in. "It looks like we

have a good case against Aldanov, and when we are ready, there will be a court case, and we will want you to give evidence against him. That will probably be a month or more away, and we'll discuss your evidence in much more detail nearer the time. But what plans do you have, Marina?"

"I suppose I just want to go back to work again and live as normal a life as possible – will that be a problem?"

"I think it will be," said Tom. "We know that the Russian embassy people are anxious to get to you and to your father, perhaps to try to influence your evidence and maybe play on your Russian background in some way. Would you say you still have what I might call Russian sympathies?"

"Not at all," she replied quickly. "Not in the political sense. It is just the history of Russia that interests me because of the family background – it would be the same wherever they came from. A lot of people are researching their ancestors on the Internet these days and discovering things they never knew."

"Yes, that's true," said Tom. "I've been doing it myself. But it is a bit different when the Russian secret service gets involved – and why do you think they want to see your father as well?"

"I'm not sure," said Marina. "He was not very forthcoming when I asked him about that in Portsmouth last Friday, but I think he was quite worried – and not just about me. I can talk to him again, if you like?"

"Sure, you can do that, but I think we will be talking to him as well. There is another problem, and that's the press. This has all become a big news story in the papers and on TV, and they all want to interview you, and we are anxious to prevent that happening because of your value to us as a witness. You can always say no, of course, but they will be very persistent and can make life difficult, as well as offering you a big fat cheque. One way forward would be to agree to your doing one exclusive interview with someone fairly reliable like the BBC, and we would help you to prepare for this. But that would only create another news story, and everything you said or didn't say would be analysed and followed up on, and all this could create a wrong impression about you when the time came for you to give evidence at the trial."

"I don't like the sound of that," said Marina. "So how can I avoid all this for a month or more?"

"I have a suggestion," said Tom. "Would you consider moving to work for us in MI5, or at least give it a try? You already work for the Government, and a transfer to the MOD in some capacity would be quite straightforward. Then when the trial is over, you could quietly move from Portsmouth to join us here in this section, perhaps on the Russian desk?"

This unexpected idea made Marina gasp in amazement. And then, for the first time, she sensed that something positive might come from all this – but then she realised that it would also mean returning to London, and she was enjoying Portsmouth so much more.

"Wow – that's an interesting idea. That would mean moving back to London, I suppose – but where would I be for the next month until the trial?" she asked.

"We have an exchange arrangement with our counterparts in the States – how would you fancy a few weeks in Florida?"

Marina's eyes lit up even more. "Are you serious?"

"They have a section there which teaches foreign languages", Tom continued. "And we could probably get you a place there to start learning Russian – perhaps as a future trainee in our section. That could be very useful to you and us in the longer term. No-one else needs to know where you are or what you are doing. In fact, it will be better if no-one knows. Who would you need to tell?"

"My parents and a few friends in Portsmouth would wonder where I was – and then there are the people at the office in the Dockyard. Then there is my flat and the neighbours there… but that's about all, I think."

"Don't worry about the Navy, we can deal with that. But for the rest, we would need to work out a good cover story with you – and you won't be surprised to know that we are quite good at that in MI5. Above all else, remember you signed the Official Secrets Act, and the department you will be visiting in America is hush-hush and top secret, not to be revealed to anyone, before or after. You will understand this better when you get there. Anyway, give all this some thought and we will catch up again later."

The long session ended, and Patricia returned to collect Marina, who was thoughtful and feeling apprehensive as they went to have lunch together in the staff restaurant. Marina was not sure how much to share with her new friend, and the American trip was never mentioned. However, it became obvious that Patricia had been briefed about the plan to offer Marina a job in London at some time in the future, and she was very encouraging and supportive. "We have a great team here, and I am sure you would love it," she said. And afterwards, she took Marina for a planned meeting with another officer in a different department who began by saying that he had "a bit of experience in arranging cover stories" and had some ideas to talk through with her.

19.
INTRODUCING "MARY"

That evening, and alone for a while, Marina had much to think about. She decided to ring her father and told him she was now in a flat in London. It had been provided by the authorities, she explained, while she was being interviewed about the Russian affair, and she asked whether he had heard anything further.

"Yes," he replied. "I am glad you called because I have been visited here today by two different reporters. They mainly wanted to find out where you were, and I couldn't tell them anything."

"Well, don't tell them," interrupted Marina.

"The press also wanted to interview me and asked me things about my background as well as yours. I just told them a few things about your early days in London and then about my business, and luckily, they were not still here a bit later on because a man from the Russian embassy arrived at the house, and that could have been difficult. I didn't tell the press anything about the calls I've had from the Russian embassy."

"So why are they interested in you, Dad?" she asked. "Have you had any dealings with them before?"

Victor Peters sounded very cautious. "Nothing important," he replied. "It's just that they have people there who like to stay in touch with me and my brother because of our background, I suppose. Just in case they can be of any help to us."

"What did he say about me and my contact with the Russian navy man?"

"Not much. Except that he wanted to know more about it and thought I would have known more from my chat with you at the weekend, but I said that my only concern was to know that you were all right – so are you? What's happening now?"

"Yes, don't worry, Dad – and tell Mum I'm OK. I really rang to let you know that I may be away for the next few weeks. The people here are very anxious that I should stay out of sight from the press and the Russians – really out of sight. So I've been in touch with an old college friend who now lives in Canada, and I'll be flying off for a holiday there in the next few days. I'll stay in touch with you when I get there, so don't worry, and please, please don't tell anybody."

Victor then handed over the phone to his wife, and Marina told her the same story and tried to be as comforting and reassuring as she could.

"I do worry about all this," said Shona Peters. "Do take care of yourself."

The next morning, Patricia was up early and over their shared breakfast of cereals and fresh fruit, Marina said she had thought more about a cover story and had worked out an idea about going to stay with an old school friend in Canada, if that would be acceptable to the boss?

Patricia thought that sounded good as she went to the office, asking Marina to wait for further news about what would happen next. By 9 am, Patricia was back at the flat and surprised Marina by handing over round-trip airline tickets to Orlando, Florida, a new passport in the name of Mary McMasters, documents for immigration and a wallet containing a credit card in Marina's new name, and a wad of US 20 and 50-dollar bills. There was also a new mobile phone.

"Pack your belongings quickly," said Patricia. "You have a flight at 11.45 this morning. Can you give me the keys to your flat in Portsmouth, and don't worry, we will make sure everything there is secure. Feel free to use the credit card and cash for any clothes or anything else you may need. It will be quite warm in Florida still. And by the way, I will take you to the airport and you will be met and looked after by our American friends when you arrive."

A somewhat bewildered Marina could only go with the flow, and within 20 minutes, a waiting car drove them to Heathrow. Patricia then stayed with Marina until she had checked in, done some essential shopping for toiletries and a current affairs magazine in the departure lounge, and chatted reassuringly as they shared a coffee until the Orlando flight was called.

Marina, now Mary McMasters, was soon trying to relax at last with a glass of orange juice in the new experience, for her, of a comfortable business class seat for her eight-hour flight.

20.
MEANWHILE IN PUTNEY

While Marina/Mary was in the air, Victor Peters had another visit at his home in Putney from the Russian embassy agent, "Jack". Shona greeted him cautiously, and when he was alone with Victor, he began by thanking him for helping them with information in the past.

"Without your help, we would not have known about your daughter's job with the British navy," he began, which rather alarmed Victor. "Jack" then went on to suggest that there could be "substantial rewards" for Victor if he could also get some further help now from his daughter. Victor realised for the first time that he been unwittingly trapped by a conversation he'd had a few months earlier at Embassy reception for expat residents in London. He now recalled saying how proud he was of his daughter and that he may have mentioned what she was doing.

He told "Jack" that he would need time to think about such an important matter, and the conversation turned to the story about the Peters family business. The subject of Marina was not raised again until the Russian was about to leave, with a reminder of the offer he had made. Shona overheard this final conversation at the door and asked her husband to tell her more because she was concerned about his contact with the persistent embassy man; she urged

Victor to take care and not get involved. Victor decided to have another chat with his brother, who had already been in touch over the weekend after reading about Marina in the newspapers.

The two brothers were now semi-retired, and their fabrics business had expanded into a chain of six shops in the southeast of England. Marina's interests had been elsewhere, and since Andrew had no family to follow them in the business, they had now recruited an experienced management team to run Peters Brothers – but they still kept an oversight of their company.

"Have you ever had any contact with the Russian embassy?" he asked Andrew, who was then at the office they shared over their main shop in South London.

"Not recently," he replied. "There was that one occasion last year when we were both invited to a reception there, but you couldn't make it and I went with my wife – do you remember that? It made me realise that they knew something about you and me and our background, but I wasn't sure why we were invited until one of the staff there started asking me about my network of friends in London – what clubs I belonged to, and so on. Did I still speak Russian?"

"They must have us both on some sort of list," said Victor. "That explains why Shona and I were invited to another party at the embassy a couple of months ago, and this time we were able to accept. I remember now that after a few drinks, one of the officers there cornered me and started asking me about you and then about our business activities and then about my family. It now seems that I must have told him something about Marina's new job in Portsmouth. They certainly knew where to find me when this latest business blew up, and I've now had two phone calls and a visit today from one of the people there who seemed to be on the intelligence side. Today, he even asked me whether I was interested in helping them, and he seemed to think I could get Marina to pass on information from her job in Portsmouth."

"I suppose they have to try everything; that's their job," replied Andrew. "What did you say?"

"I didn't want to just say no in case it rebounded on me or Marina in some way. I just said I would think about it. I don't want to get involved in anything like this. He was really pressing me to tell him where Marina is. What do you think?"

"Just be very careful, Victor. And where is Marina now?"

"As far as I know, she is still helping the police put together the case against that Russian naval man. I don't know any more than that, except that she called today to say that she was going to be away for a few days – and not to say a word to anyone."

They agreed to catch up later at the office, and Victor was just preparing to go to the office to join his brother when his phone rang.

"Mr. Peters?" a voice said. "My name is Tom Spencer – I work for the Government security service, and I have been chatting to your daughter, Marina. Do you think I could come to see you sometime today? I can be there in about 30 minutes."

"Yes, of course," said Victor. "I'll be pleased to see you to find out what is going on."

Shona was curious. "This time it's someone from the British security service," explained Victor. "He wants to come here in half an hour, and I hope he can tell us more about everything and where Marina is. Let's wait to see what he has to say."

Tom duly arrived at the Peters' home in Putney, showed his credentials and greeted Victor and Shona warmly. He declined the offer of a drink or a cup of tea and began by apologising for encouraging Marina to go away for a few weeks.

"It is very important for us to keep her away from the press or any other outside influences while we work on this case against the Russian, so we were very happy when she said she has found a friend to visit in Canada. In fact, she is already on the way today. But please do not tell anyone where she has gone," he insisted.

"Canada?" replied a surprised Victor and Shona gave a gasp. "We didn't know she was in touch with a friend there, did we Shona?"

"Not that I can remember," she said. "This seems very sudden but we are getting a lot of surprises these days".

Victor added: "Yes, we are not sure what is going on and as it happens, I've had several press people calling up and asking where she is. And then a man from the Russian embassy came here just this morning asking the same question, but I could not tell them any details, anyway, because I didn't know."

"So what else did the Russian want – and do you know who he is?"

"Not really. He gave me a phone number to call and said ask for Jack."

"Well, I work with MI5 as it happens, and I imagine you know what that is?" Tom continued, and Victor nodded. "Well, we are carrying out an important inquiry into whether this Russian navy man is actually a secret agent and whether he tricked Marina into a relationship to try to get information from her – you know she was doing confidential work for the Navy in Portsmouth, of course? And your family background and Russian connections make this of real concern to us."

"I don't think you have any worries on that account," said Victor. "My parents and now my brother and I are very grateful for the way we have been able to live our lives in Britain, and we feel very British. In fact, it seemed to me to be a sort of acceptance of this when Marina was taken on by the Royal Navy. We are very proud of that."

"Thank you for that assurance, Mr. Peters. We also know that there are a couple of thousand Russian emigres in London and that the intelligence service at the Russian embassy relies on quite a few of them as informants of one sort or another. We have to keep a close eye on them, and we are aware that you and your brother are known to the embassy and appear on their files, but so far as I know, your family is not under any sort of suspicion. This situation with your daughter is the first time that your names have been highlighted, but we still have to take it seriously. Did your visitor today say anything else?"

"He suggested in a roundabout way that I could possibly be of help to him – perhaps by passing on any information I might get from Marina – and I didn't like the sound of that. After he left, I chatted to my brother Andrew and we agreed that we did not want anything to do with him. If I hear from him again, I will tell him just that, unless you think it could put Marina in any sort of danger?"

"Don't worry about that – we will take good care of Marina. Have you had any other contacts with the Russian embassy?"

"Not really," replied Victor. "My wife and I went to a reception at the embassy earlier this year, and it seemed that they like to stay in touch with people such as my brother and me who are in business here – just a social thing, that's all."

Shona then asked, "Is Marina quite safe, Mr. Spencer? Is she in any sort of trouble? This all sounds very worrying."

"No, no," said Tom. "You can rely on our team to make sure this all works out. She is helping us in many ways, and we are discovering that your daughter is a bright and intelligent lady; we are all very impressed by her."

Victor and Shona appreciated this, and Tom then changed the subject. They all relaxed as they chatted about the Peters' successful business, and he admired their lovely home and their choice of Putney, near the river, for their retirement years.

"Well, it was good to meet you, Mr. and Mrs. Peters," said Tom, getting up to leave. "Let me know if you hear anything further from this Jack fellow, and I will let you know how Marina is getting on. I assure you that she is not in any sort of trouble. It is just that she will be our key witness when the Russian comes to trial as a spy, so she is very important to us."

He left, and a couple of minutes later, the doorbell rang again. This time, it was a man who introduced himself as a reporter from the Daily Star, who apologised for intruding and asked, "Was that another reporter who just left here?"

"No, no," said Victor. "It was a friend, and I really don't want to talk to the press any more. You are the third today."

The reporter was persistent and insisted that he just wanted to check a few facts if Victor could spare him a few minutes. Victor reluctantly invited him into the house. He explained that after the brief court appearance by the Russian, his editor wanted him to discover more background details about Marina and her family. Victor could not resist and began to describe how his parents had emigrated from Russia in the 1930s to search for a better life in England; how they had been helped at first by other Russians living in East London; how they had started their own business; how they had become British citizens in 1945; and how their two sons had then expanded their small shop in South London into the Peters Brothers business which now supplied fabrics to some of the best couturiers and designers in London.

The reporter began to warm to this story, with the Russian family angle fitting well as a follow up to the story of the forthcoming trial appearance of Nikolai Aldanov. For his questions about Marina, he found Victor to be more reluctant to answer. He quickly suspected that the police or MI5 had told him not to pass on any information and asked, "Is Marina in custody? Has she been charged with anything?"

"I really can't tell you anything more," said Victor. "As far as I know, she is the main witness in the case they are bringing against the Russian, and they don't want her to talk about it before the trial. I spoke to her earlier today, and she is fine, and I think she is going away to stay with a friend for a few days."

"Any idea where she is?"

"No, she thought it would be better if I didn't know, so that's all I can say today."

They said their farewells, and the reporter drove off, quite happy with the story he had now gleaned about Marina's family links with Russia. This would become another exclusive feature for the Daily Star the next day.

21.
IT'S DISNEYWORLD

Marina's flight landed in sunny Florida in the late afternoon, local time. She had been able to unwind a little at last and enjoy the business class service – but she cautiously limited herself to just one glass of white wine. During the eight-hour flight, she managed to get some sleep as well as watching a movie in a futile attempt to calm her anxieties about what lay ahead. She had no real idea about what to expect next as she walked down the ramp with the rest of the passengers and into the international arrivals area of the terminal. All the signs around the building were welcoming her to the World of Disney, reminding her that she had arrived in the land of Mickey Mouse. Her new passport and immigration documents were checked without question. With only carry-on luggage, she was quickly through the customs formalities and wondered what welcome awaited Mary McMasters.

She did not have long to wait. As she emerged through the doors into the arrivals hall, she spotted a large card bearing her new name. There were two men waiting for her. One of them was ready to take her luggage and was somewhat surprised to find she did not have any – just her carry-on bag. They introduced themselves as Joe and Don and led her to a waiting car, a large SUV with blackened rear windows, parked right at the door of the terminal building, with the driver poised to open the trunk and car door. There was no requirement for luggage in the trunk, so they climbed in, with Joe accompanying her in the back seats.

"How was the flight, Miss McMasters?" he asked as they drove off.

"Just fine, thanks," replied Marina, adjusting to her new name. "Thank you for meeting me. Can you tell me where we are going now?"

"OK," replied Joe. "Here's the plan. We are taking you to the Ritz Carlton hotel in town, about a 30-minute drive, and we will introduce you to one of our Deputy Directors who will be waiting there – she's Sally-Ann Waters, and she will be taking care of you during your visit. I will also stick around for a while in case there is anything you need. I am calling her now to give her our ETA."

As they drove, Marina was overwhelmed by the huge signboards and neon displays along the highway, advertising all the attractions of the Disney empire. It was certainly another world she had just stepped into. When they arrived, the hotel entrance and reception area were also mind-blowing, with their bright lights and luxurious décor. Joe took her through to a relatively quiet bar area to meet Sally-Ann.

"It's so good to see you, Mary," she said with outstretched arms. "Welcome to the Colonies. I've heard so much about you. You're looking great, but I guess you're a bit tired after that long flight."

Somehow, Sally-Ann was exactly what Marina had expected from her limited knowledge of American businesswomen in films and on TV – slim, smart, blonde and confident. Then, with a crisp and clear accent, she asked Joe: "Where's Ms. McMasters' luggage? Take it to her room."

"This is it," replied Marina, pointing to her carry-on. "I left in such a hurry this morning that I only have my overnight bag. I was told to buy everything I need when I get here."

"OK, we can handle that," said a rather surprised Sally-Ann. "Joe, go and get Ms. McMasters checked in and bring back her room key." Then turning to Marina, she continued: "Let's have a quick chat here, then maybe you would prefer to get to your room and order something to eat from room service before catching up on some sleep. We have a nice programme worked out for you over the next two or three weeks – nothing too strenuous, so don't worry – and we can go over it tomorrow morning at the office. There are some decent shops here in the hotel where you can probably find anything you need, either tonight or tomorrow."

"This all sounds wonderful," said Marina. "What do I need in the way of clothes? How warm is it here, and will I need office-type things or is it more casual?"

"We are not too formal in the CIA," said Sally-Ann. "Tee-shirts and pants are normal for most of us, and you may need a light sweater or jacket in the air-conditioning. Outside, it is pretty warm by your standards – maybe around 25 degrees during the day."

"Did you just say the CIA?" interrupted Marina. "I recognise that name. I didn't realise that I was going to be looked after by the CIA – that sounds a bit serious. Is this all very hush-hush?"

"Don't worry, Mary – it is just that we are the American cousins of the folk who you were working with in the UK."

"OK, I think I understand. What will be happening next?"

"Joe will come by at around 8.30 in the morning, and he'll drive you to our offices to meet everyone and to go through your programme. Then everything will be clear, I hope. We've had a full briefing from your folks in London, so we know what is going on there and what your needs are.

There's nothing to worry about. Here's Joe now with your room details – sleep well and see you tomorrow."

Joe took Marina with her overnight bag to the lift, handed over her key, told her to go to the 8th floor and find room 808 – "and see you tomorrow."

The room was not difficult to find, but Marina was wide-eyed as she entered it. It was spacious and luxurious, with a huge king-size bed and a bathroom twice the size of any she had ever seen. All the facilities were new and shiny, the furnishings were modern, with a 3-seater settee in front of an enormous TV, a fully-stocked minibar and a small kitchenette with all the necessaries for making hot drinks. It was almost too much to take in.

It was still only 6 pm in Orlando, but it had been a long day, and Marina decided that any shopping could wait for the morning when she would probably be awake early, anyway.

She took a look at the room service menu and picked up the phone. "Good evening Miss McMasters," came the instant reply. "Welcome to the Ritz Carlton. How can I help you?" She ordered a club sandwich, was persuaded to add a portion of "fries" and chose an ice cream dessert to follow. Within ten minutes, there was a knock at the door, and the tray was brought in and laid carefully on the table at the window, with the bright lights of Orlando spread out beyond.

This is the life, thought Marina!

Next morning, after a good sleep, jet-lag meant that she was wide awake by 5 am. After making a cup of tea and relaxing with the TV news for a while, she decided it was time to go in search of breakfast. After taking the lift to the reception area, she first discovered the parade of shops, including two with women's wear, that indicated that they would be open at 8 am. Then she found the breakfast buffet with its range of familiar and less familiar choices. After a selection of fruit and yogurt, she went back again to try the Belgian waffles with strawberries and maple syrup. It was all so tempting, but there were also new clothes to try on shortly.

She was the first customer in the shop, and she explained that her luggage had been lost somewhere *en route* from the UK and she needed a couple of new outfits for some business meetings. A very helpful assistant brought out several options to choose from and Marina soon found two which suited very well, together with the necessary accessories. Her new credit card worked, and she then found a small suitcase in a neighbouring shop, reasonably priced, which she might also need, and she returned to her room to get dressed for "work".

She was just about ready when the phone rang. It was Joe calling from reception to say that he was ready to go, and he added, "Bring your bags down with you because we'll be checking you out before we move on to the next stage. Is that OK?"

Marina tried hard not to sound too disappointed to be leaving her luxury room so soon; she did as she was asked as quickly as possible and then went down to meet Joe. He had already dealt with the check-out desk and signing for her room – and Marina realised she had no idea what such luxury had cost the CIA! Then, taking her new luggage, he led her out to the waiting car. Marina wondered anxiously, and not for the first time, "What next?"

The car soon left the city streets and headed past a series of hoardings attracting traffic to the various Disney locations before reaching the residential suburbs and then a less developed area with fruit farms and eventually a gated entrance with the sign reading "United States Government: Camp Orchard".

After being checked briefly by the security guards, they drove another half mile through what appeared to be apple orchards to reach a large building in traditional plantation house style, with white columns either side of the elegant porch and steps. At the door, they were met by Sally-Ann Waters, who greeted "Mary" warmly with a welcome to Camp Orchard. It all seemed surprisingly relaxed and friendly.

"Would you take Miss McMasters' luggage to Block C?" she instructed Joe, briskly. "She will be in room two and bring the key back to me in the conference room."

Sally-Ann then described some of the features of the house to her visitor as they walked through the elegant hallway and corridors to reach a room which immediately looked more formal and business-like, with its conference table and chairs plus a range of electronic equipment and computer screens. There were two men waiting there who were introduced as the Director of Camp Orchard, Charles Rooney, and the Head of Research, Robert Chilton – both looking relaxed in jeans, cowboy boots and button-down shirts.

"Hi, Mary," said the Director. "Call me Chuck. It's great to have you here. We've had a full briefing from London, so we know all about you, and we don't need to go into all that anymore. We just want you to enjoy your time with us and make a few new friends – and maybe learn a few useful things, as well. You've already met Sally-Ann, of course, and she will stay in contact with you for anything you might need to know. Bob, here, is in charge of the group you will be joining later. Any questions, Mary?"

"Nothing I can think of now," replied Marina. The Director said, "Good luck," and left the room. Joe arrived with the room key, which Sally-Ann handed over with a brief "see you later", and she departed, as well.

"Right, Mary," said Robert Chilton, without wasting any time. "We've got a small group of six new agents in training here – two gals and four guys – and they started just yesterday on a four-week language course in basic Russian. We'll join them a bit later. They're a good bunch, five American ex-servicemen and one from Canada, and they've done nearly six months with the department, covering a variety of training courses here and overseas. They are all destined to join our Russian section in DC very soon and need to have an understanding of the language, like you. Do you have any Russian yourself?"

"Not really," she replied. "My family came from Russia two generations ago, and they have all become pretty well anglicised. I suppose I've picked up a few words here and there but nothing that would be useful."

"We use a mixture of methods here, Mary, starting with some basic classroom sessions to learn about grammar and reading and pronunciation. Then you will go on to the language laboratory where there will be sessions of conversation with recordings and playback until you find yourself feeling quite familiar with hearing and understanding the Russian voice. Then, by the third week, we will have the entire group talking nothing but Russian to each other – you will be surprised how quickly it catches on. You'll be dreaming in Russian before you know it. The final stage is to have you all reading and understanding documents in Russian. How does that sound?"

"Pretty terrifying, but I suppose it works."

"OK, then let's go to meet the group and the instructor in charge."

22.
A BOMBSHELL!

Back at the MI5 headquarters in London, Tom Spencer called his team together again.

"I want to take a closer look at Victor Peters," he began. "I went to his home to meet him yesterday, and he had all the right answers. But I think he may be hiding something. He certainly has some links with the Russian embassy and may turn out to be an informer, even before his daughter got mixed up with Aldanov."

The meeting went on to review their work to date, and the lawyers confirmed that the case against Aldanov was coming together well but that it would need extremely convincing evidence from Marina for it to stand up in court. His past history with GRU in Moscow did not suggest any involvement with the UK until he reported his online contact, and he clearly thought he could enhance his reputation by following up his honey trap in person.

The agents who had been digging into Marina's past reported that they had not come up with anything to suggest that she had any nefarious ambitions. In fact, among all her friends from schooldays onwards, none of them knew about her Russian background or that she had any special interest in politics or international affairs. Previous boyfriends had found her to be serious-minded, quite reserved and certainly not flirtatious, and they had all been surprised to read the story in the news about her contact with the Russian. It had seemed "out of character" for her to follow up a relationship for so long, even one at a distance.

Tom listened to the reports from around the table and emphasized that when Marina returned from the trip to the US, they would need to spend time preparing her evidence carefully. Then he surprised the meeting with a bombshell.

"Now, this is only an idea at this stage," he confided, "but the Foreign Office have asked us to consider whether Aldanov might be a suitable candidate for an exchange deal for one of our diplomats who is under house arrest in Moscow because they suspected him of some undercover activity. If they bring charges against our man, it could be a bit embarrassing for the FO, and they think a swap might be a way to pre-empt some future problems.

"One factor we have to consider with the FO is whether this would work better before we put Aldanov on trial here – in which case, we would not need Marina's testimony anyway. Based on past experience, it takes quite a while to set up this sort of exchange with the Russians, and if it goes ahead, it needs to be handled very, very carefully. But it will be their call, not ours.

"And there's something else," he continued. "We are also giving some careful thought here to the future of Marina Peters and whether she and possibly her father could become useful to us when all this business dies down. She will certainly gain some useful experience during her time with the CIA boys in Florida. These decisions are out of our hands, of course. They will all be worked out upstairs – but I needed to share this with you now because it affects the way we proceed."

Tom ended the meeting by instructing the team to continue their preparatory work for the trial of Aldanov as already planned, as well as an in-depth investigation of both the Peters brothers and their associates. But he emphasised that they should advise him immediately if they heard any developments which might become a factor in the new matters he had just introduced.

23.
LEARNING RUSSIAN

At Camp Orchard, "Mary" soon settled into an easy-going routine. Her room was comfortably furnished and equipped – not quite the Ritz Carlton but better than she expected in a government facility. There was an adjoining study room with books and computers, and in the main building, the restaurant was modern and attractive, and the food choices were excellent. The swimming pool was adjacent to the accommodation block, together with a sauna and a games room. So there were no complaints.

The company proved good, too. The group of seven were soon on warm and friendly terms, and the two women classmates soon arranged to take "Mary" on visits to some of the tourist attractions at the weekend – including Disney World, Seaworld and Epcot. Late on her first evening there, feeling a little homesick, she thought she should call her father, but her new phone did not appear to have a signal. After breakfast the next morning, she went in search of Sally-Ann in the administrative offices and told her about the problem.

"Sorry about that," explained Sally-Ann. "But we do not have any open communications here for security reasons. Everything is screened through our comms centre, and your London folk told me that you should not make a call from here to your home. Your father's lines are probably being monitored by now, and the Russians could easily trace where any call is coming from; you are not supposed to be in Florida, or any place connected with the CIA.

"Can I suggest that you use one of our protected circuits in the office to call another friend in England who is not involved in this business and then ask them to contact your father with a reassuring message – and to say you are in Canada, of course. Would that work for you?"

"I don't see why not. I have a good friend in Portsmouth called Betty McGuire, who could do this, and I will work out my cover story about being in Canada."

"Fine – unless your friend also works for the Navy. That could be a bit difficult."

"No, she's a hospital nurse," Marina said.

"That should be okay then. I'll fix a time when you can come back here later to make a call. There's a five-hour time difference, of course, so maybe early afternoon would be a good time here to reach your friend in the morning, perhaps?"

"Mary" agreed and went to join the group for their first classroom session of the day. After the lunch break, she was called to go to the office, and she gave the comms officer the number of her friend Betty. She was taken to a private phone booth and given instructions on what to do next. A few minutes later, she was told to pick up the phone and could hear the number ringing.

"Hello, this is Betty – who's calling?"

"It's Marina – how are you and what's going on there?"

"Well, hi Marina. Lovely to hear your voice. You sound good – how's the holiday?"

"Oh, it's a really nice break – and I needed it. I'm with a friend in Canada, and I'll tell you all about it when I get back. I also wanted to call Dad, but I couldn't get through, and I don't want to make too many long-distance calls from here. So I wonder if you could ring him in Putney for me – do you have his number?"

"Gosh – you are in Canada – and so quickly! And yes, of course, what shall I tell him?"

"Just say I wanted to let him know that I have arrived safely here in Quebec and that all is well. My friend is looking after me, and there's lots to see and do. The flight over was good, and there's nothing to worry about. I will probably stay a couple of weeks. That's about all…"

"Can I give him a number to call you back."

"No, that's not really necessary. I will probably be out and about quite a lot, and then there's the time difference. Just say I'll try to call again next week."

"OK, I will do that … but what are you up to there? The papers are still running stories about your meeting with a Russian spy, and there has been an interesting piece about your father and his business. Sounds like he has done well. With the press nosing around, it is probably a good idea that you are away for a couple of weeks."

"That was the plan, Betty. The authorities there did not want me to be bothered by the press until I had given evidence against the Russian at his trial. Apparently, he is really a spy and not just the naval officer I thought he was. He really led me on, and I am quite embarrassed by all the discussions we had on the website."

"I'm not surprised. He really looks quite nice in the pictures they have in the paper. Anyway, how's Canada?"

"A bit cold, but nice sunny days and there's lots to see. I'll tell you all about it another time."

"OK Marina, I'll look forward to that, and I'll give your dad a call this evening. Take care of yourself."

"And you too, Betty. See you soon – bye."

With that job done, Marina relaxed and felt she could

now focus on enjoying Florida and hopefully learning some Russian conversation phrases.

The next two weeks went quite quickly. The classroom sessions were intensive but effective, and at the weekend, the three girls were ready to escape to see the wonderful performing dolphins at Seaworld, followed by a day at Epcot, where Marina was disappointed to find that among all the amazing national displays, there was still no Russian pavilion. During her third week at Camp Orchard, just as she was becoming familiar with the conversation sessions, Marina was called to the office to see Director Rooney.

"Hi Mary", he began. "I've just had an interesting talk with Tom Spencer in London – you know him, of course? Well, he now wants you back there next week – how does that sound?"

"That's sooner than I expected, but I guess there's a good reason. Just when I was starting to enjoy myself here," laughed Marina.

"We'll be sorry to see you go," he said. "We like having a Brit with us for a change. Anyway, could you give Sally-Ann your travel documents, and we will try to fix you a flight on Friday so that you can rest up for the weekend at home before getting back with Tom and his chums next week."

"Do you know what this is about?" asked Marina. "And where do I go when I arrive in London. Can you ask them for me?"

"I can do better than that. Let's get Tom on the line, and you can have a chat with him."

An assistant scuttled away and after a couple of minutes came back with the news that Mr. Spencer was on line one. The Director opened up the speaker phone and began. "It's Chuck here again, Tom, and I have your nice lady with us to have a word. Is that okay?"

"Hello, that's fine," came a familiar British voice. "Hi Marina, how are they treating you there?"

"Very well, thanks – but now I'm told it's time to come back."

"Yes, we are making good progress here, and now we would like to spend some time with you again. When can you make it?"

"They're hoping to get me on a Friday flight so that I can recover at the weekend and then be with you on Monday. How does that sound?"

"That'll work out okay. Let me know what flight you are on, and we'll arrange to meet you at Heathrow. Is that okay?"

"Where do I go, and what happens next? And by the way, I think I left the keys to my flat with Patricia, just in case you needed to check on anything while I was away."

"Don't worry. I'll make sure that Patricia has your keys for you. When you arrive, we'll put you up at the flat here on Thameside again for the weekend, and then we can sort things out on Monday."

"One other thing, Mr. Spencer," continued Marina. "I realised the other day that I came away without saying anything to my solicitors in Portsmouth who had been so helpful. Can someone there let them know what is happening?"

"No problem, Marina. I think your police friends in Portsmouth have done that, and they have also kept in touch with your people in the Dockyard. Everyone knows that you are having a nice break in Canada until things settle down again. OK? See you next Monday, then."

24.
"MARY" RETURNS

On the Wednesday afternoon, just three weeks after the Russian ships had arrived in Portsmouth, there was another senior-level meeting at the Home Office involving the Foreign Office, Scotland Yard, MI5 and MI6. Top of the agenda was to review the Aldanov case and decide on the next steps, and it began with the elegant Oliver Anderson-Scott from the FO leading the way with a surprise announcement.

"We have been having some back-channel exchanges with our contacts at GRU and at the Russian Embassy, and it seems that our little plan may be working out," he stated. "You may not have known that when we saw the chance to pick up this Aldanov chappie in Portsmouth last month, we had another agenda in mind regarding one of our attachés being held by the Ruskies in Moscow. We have kept this matter very low profile while we tried to find out more, and it appears that they were anxious to keep it quiet, too. His name is Charles Alexander, and they said he had been caught outside the Moscow city limits – as you know, our people have to get special permission to do that. They also claimed that he had been caught taking pictures of one of the latest antennas used by their air defences around the capital. Our fellows in the Moscow embassy have kept us in the picture, of course, but no-one is saying very much – he is under house arrest and has been interviewed several times by the GRU, but it does not seem to be going any further at present.

"So, at one of the meetings where we answered their regular questions about our intentions regarding Aldanov, our people found the right moment to drop the subject of Alexander's detention into the discussion – and cautiously, they introduced the idea of a swap. The Russians would not commit themselves at first, as usual, but now we have good reason to believe that we could make it work. I suspect that they don't want the story about their defence antennas to get any attention, and I think they are also nervous about Aldanov going on trial with some spicy evidence about his relationship with the girl – and maybe more. They don't know what he might say. What has happened to her, by the way?"

Tom then explained that not only had the world's press been eager to interview her but that a Russian couple had suddenly turned up in Portsmouth looking for her. They had been photographed by the local CID, and it had been possible to identify them as known GRU agents based at the Russian embassy in London. Also, the Russian embassy had sent someone to see the girl's father and tried to put pressure on him. So it had been decided that Marina Peters should be kept out of sight for a while, and it had been arranged for her to travel to Florida with a new identity to spend a few weeks at the CIA Languages School to learn Russian.

Sir Oliver pondered this information for a minute or two and then delivered his decision.

"You know, I think we can do without a show trial as well. Let's see if we can get this exchange plan under way, and then you can bring the girl back from the States because she will not be needed to give evidence. What do you all think?"

The lawyers and MI6 agents who had spent many hours preparing the case against Aldanov tried to conceal their disappointment, but they nodded their agreement, as did the others at the meeting. They then turned to the question of Victor Peters and the extent to which he might have been complicit in the affair by informing his Russian friends about his daughter's work for the Navy. The representative from the Security Service said they had now been monitoring all of Victor Peters' activities for several weeks and had researched his records and there were certainly suspicions about his relationships with Russian embassy staff. It was agreed that this close surveillance should be continued and reviewed again after the Aldanov matter had been concluded.

There was nothing else on the agenda, and before the meeting broke up, there was a final insistence from Anderson-Scott of the FO that nothing regarding the proposed spy exchange should be leaked until it could be officially announced by the Foreign Office – and that this would be *after* it had been successfully concluded.

The next morning, Tom received a call from his boss, directing him to call the CIA without delay to bring an end to Marina's trip and for her to be available for a de-briefing on Monday. After his calls to Chuck and his chat with Marina, Tom set the wheels in motion and soon received a message from Florida with the return flight arrangements. He briefed his associate, Patricia, to meet the flight and to liaise with immigration so that she could pick up her contact at the aircraft door and escort her through the special security section in the VIP arrivals area so that there would be no confusion with her two identities. When a confidential message arrived confirming Marina's arrival at Terminal 5 at 10 am on Saturday, Patricia replied to confirm that she would be there to welcome her back and take her to the Thameside apartment again for the weekend.

Everything went just as planned. "Mary" was given a farewell party in the office before she was driven off to Orlando airport. She managed to get some sleep during the overnight flight back to London. As she left the plane, she was delighted to see the familiar face of Patricia waiting to welcome her and take her to a special lounge where they completed the formalities with an immigration official and reunited her with her luggage. Eventually, when she was able to relax in the back of the official car, heading into London on the M4, she asked Patricia the question that had been on her mind for the past two days: "So what happens next?"

Patricia could only reply, "There's a lot going on, Marina, and Tom says he will brief us all at a meeting on Monday. I think you should be able to call your family and friends from the flat over the weekend and tell them what a lovely time you had in Canada. There's been some more stuff in the press while you've been away, but mostly about your Dad and some more guesswork about what the Russian guy, Aldanov, had in mind. You are still the mystery lady in all this, and we want you to stay that way for another few days."

Patricia and the driver took Marina and her luggage back to what was now the familiar 8th-floor flat. This time, Patricia was not staying there as well, and after just a few minutes of chatting, she prepared to leave, saying, "Just call me on my mobile if you need anything – but have a good rest, and I will come to collect you at about nine on Monday morning for the meeting with Tom at the office."

Marina quickly asked whether she would be able to contact her parents and possibly go to Putney over the weekend to see them, perhaps for Sunday lunch? Patricia said she would check this out and let her know if this was a problem. Then she explained that the press and the Russian embassy had all been visiting her father, so she thought it might be better if she arranged to meet them somewhere else in London. This would enable one of their agents to keep an eye on her – "just in case you are recognised."

25.
NO SPYING TRIAL

During a restful Saturday, Marina rang her parents, who were surprised and delighted to know that she was safely back in London – and even more excited by the prospect of getting together, at last, the next day. But otherwise, Marina had a quiet evening and an early night to readjust her time clock.

As Patricia had suggested, the Sunday lunch was booked by Victor Peters at a West End hotel; it was just the opportunity for Marina to catch up on all the events of the past few weeks with her father and mother and to reassure them, repeatedly, that she was not in any kind of trouble. Luckily, she had done enough online research about Quebec to be able to chat about the province, the weather and Canada in general. Victor Peters went on to tell his daughter about the visits he had received while she was away – from the Russian Embassy, from MI5 and from several reporters – and she apologised for being the cause of so much trouble. It was clear that he and his brother were actually quite flattered by the story in the paper about the success of Peters Brothers and how the business had been started by their father, a penniless refugee from Russia in the 1930s.

"And I told them all how proud I was of your successes over the years and how it had just been your friendly nature which had led to all this business with the Russian officer," he added.

"What did the man from the Russian embassy want?" she enquired.

"He was only interested in discovering where you were so that he could hear your side of the story about meeting the man from the Russian Navy ship. There was nothing I could tell him, so that was the end of that."

Marina again sensed that there was more to her father's connections with the Russian Embassy than he was telling her, so she changed the subject, and they went on to talk more about her trip to Canada and various family matters. She also sensed that a man dining alone, two tables away and reading his Sunday papers, was also keeping an eye on them – but he was "one of ours", she decided, remembering Patricia's advice. After a couple of hours together and a traditional English Sunday lunch, and with the excuse of jetlag, she said she needed to get some sleep before an important meeting the next day.

Back at the flat, she had a long phone chat with her friend Betty and said she hoped to be able to return to Portsmouth very soon, as soon as the trial of the Russian was over; she was hoping to hear news about this in a day or two.

"I'm assuming this is why I was asked to come back now," she added – remembering to add that there had been much more of Canada she still wanted to see.

The kitchen in the apartment still had the basic supplies, with fresh milk and juice in the fridge and several frozen meals in the freezer. After a light meal and a good night's sleep, Marina awoke in time to get breakfast, feeling somewhat apprehensive about the next stage in her saga of unexpected events. Patricia called soon after 8 am and duly arrived at her door at 9 am; they walked together to the MI5 headquarters in the Thameside building.

Tom and two of his colleagues were waiting in a conference room, and they all gave Marina a cheerful welcome back – with a joke about getting her own name back and another about how she had got a suntan in Canada. Then Tom began the meeting.

"A few things have been happening while you were away, Marina, and it was really useful that you were not being hounded by the press – or even the Russians – because it has been a sensitive time for all of us. The bottom line is that there is not going to be a trial and you won't have to give evidence after all."

Marina's eyes widened, and she gave an audible sigh of relief as Tom continued:

"This is all very hush-hush, of course, but in the next couple of days, Nikolai Aldanov will be flown out of the country. We have arranged to do a spy swap with the Russians, exchanging him for one of our diplomats who has been detained in Moscow for nearly two months on a false suspicion of spying. As it turns out, this is an arrangement which suits both sides – not least because the Russians would be very embarrassed if all the details of your online relationship with Aldanov came out in court. I don't think that would really be any good for us, either – or for you. And we get our man back as well, which will be good news for the Foreign Office. How does that sound?"

"Well, that is all very unexpected," said Marina, slowly and thoughtfully. "I had no idea that it might work out like this, but I must say it's a big relief. Obviously, the thought of giving evidence against Nikolai has been on my mind constantly, and I kept thinking about how I would handle any cross-examination because he would be there listening and looking at me. I now realise that I was quite stupid in telling him so much personal stuff. So what will happen next?"

Tom replied, "As soon as we have confirmation that

Aldanov is on his way to Moscow, I think you can relax and go back to your parents' home or back to Portsmouth, as you wish. We have stayed in touch with your people in the Navy, and although they don't know any of this latest plan, they have said that your job there is waiting for you when you are ready."

"When the swap is completed, the Foreign Office will put out a statement to explain what has happened and why Aldanov will not face a trial in this country. It is inevitable that when that happens, the press will be after you again. Patricia will arrange for you to have a session with our PR people later today or tomorrow to advise you on how to handle it, what you can say and what you can't say. Does that sound okay?"

"Yes, of course, and thank you. I understand," replied Marina, who had tears in her eyes as she left the meeting with Patricia and walked to the staff canteen for a welcome cup of coffee.

26.
THE SPY SWAP

Very early on the following morning, a surprised and bewildered Nikolai Aldanov was taken from his prison cell by two armed escorts to a waiting van and was driven out of the city to Northolt military airport, where they all boarded a waiting plane. As it took off into the dawn sky, he had no idea where he was heading. Was it for more questioning? By whom? Even Guantanamo Bay flashed through his mind.

At about the same time in Moscow, Charles Alexander was woken up by the doorbell ringing insistently at his bachelor flat – one of many rented by the British Embassy for diplomats. His visitor, a Russian army officer, said in his best broken English, "Pack your luggage, we are leaving in one hour."

Charles was also bewildered, assuming that his house arrest was being replaced by a prison cell or even worse. He dressed, found his suitcases and started packing his belongings as quickly as he could. The Russian officer watched to see whether he was taking anything other than his clothes and toiletries. He was told to leave his laptop computer, and his briefcase was searched before he was allowed to take it – fortunately Embassy rules did not allow staff to take any confidential material away from the office. Then, with no formality, he was escorted down to the street and helped into a waiting black vehicle with an armed guard.

A dozen horrific thoughts flashed through his mind as he was driven away at speed through the morning traffic with sirens screaming.

After about 30 minutes, he could see that he was arriving at a well-guarded military establishment and was surprised to see, soon afterwards, that it was an airfield. The vehicle stopped by a Russian air force transport plane. He was hustled on board to a bleak seating area with just four uncomfortable canvas seats and found himself seated between two stern-looking Russians in civilian clothes, who remained incommunicative, apart from grunting a few words to each other from time to time.

At around midday, two planes landed within ten minutes of each other at a Finnish air force base not far from Helsinki. Waiting there in a small terminal building were senior intelligence chiefs from the local embassies of Russia and Great Britain, who had been through this process a few times before. Aldanov and Alexander were each brought into the building by their escorts, together with their belongings – the British man with his two suitcases and a briefcase, the Russian with just a plastic bag containing the few items he had with him in his prison cell in London. They stood, one at each end of the room, as the officials went through the procedures of checking the identities of the two men. Little was said until they were each told to walk forward. As they passed each other, in the middle of the room, they exchanged glances and half-smiles which spoke volumes – "free at last."

Each was greeted by a handshake from his own Government representative, and with few words being spoken, they were each escorted to the aircraft which would take them home. They realised that they had been involved in a very efficient, if rather scary, diplomatic swap, and as they relaxed in their aircraft seats ready for take-off, they

The Russian Lieutenant

both wanted to cheer and say thank you – but in both cases, there were only the military escorts plus the respective aircrews on board, going busily about their duties.

For each of them, their flights back – one to Northolt and the other to Moscow with no more than a cup of aircrew coffee – were an opportunity to at least thank their lucky stars and prepare for the welcome that would await them when they landed.

Later the same day, the Foreign Office issued its press release which astonished the editors who received it in London and across the country:

"In a co-operative arrangement with the Russian Government, it has proved possible to carry out an exchange today of a Russian agent who was arrested in Portsmouth two months ago with a British diplomat who has been under house arrest in Moscow for some three months.

The exchange took place at an airfield in Finland, and we are grateful to the Finnish Government for their assistance in enabling this operation to take place.

Those involved were Charles Alexander, a member of the diplomatic service, who had been serving at the British Embassy in Moscow until he was arrested on false spying charges, and Nikolai Aldanov, the Russian agent who was arrested when he arrived in Portsmouth on board the RS Admiral Essen. We are pleased to welcome Mr. Alexander back home after his ordeal, and he will resume his duties at the Foreign Office in due course."

The news editors of London's national press and the various broadcasting organisations quickly recognised this as the final stage of the long-running story about the Russian lieutenant and his girlfriend – and instructions went out again to "find the girl."

27.
BACK HOME

After her final meeting with MI5 on Monday morning, Marina was met again by Patricia, and over a coffee in the canteen, Patricia said that Tom had asked her to pass on a message that he had been serious when he had mentioned a possible future for her with the intelligence service if she was still interested. She added, "He says we should let the dust settle for a month or two, and then we will be in touch. Meanwhile, if you have the time, he said have a few more Russian lessons."

They then went together to the office of an officer who was introduced as Dennis Winters, the information officer at MI5, who outlined the way in which Marina should deal with any press inquiries in the coming days and weeks. "Just stick to the facts that you got caught up in all this because you were looking on line for friends and that you had no idea that your contact was anything other than a naval officer," he explained. "You can insist there was no thought of secret information passing between the two of you and that you were disappointed by the way it worked out. And now you are returning to your job with the Royal Navy. Just stick to that, and I will leave it to you how much personal information you want to share."

Marina said she understood and asked a few questions

about how much information had already appeared in the press? Mr. Winters summarised the statements that had been issued and added that there had also been quite a lot of speculation. He also said she would get quite a lot of calls asking for interviews and might also be offered a payment for her exclusive story. It would be entirely up to her to decide how to respond, but to remember that her role in the whole affair was very "low level" as far as the department was concerned. "The less you say, the easier it will be," he said finally.

As they left, Patricia remembered to give Marina the keys to her flat in Portsmouth and said they had not been needed. Then, with a friendly hug, she said goodbye and wished her well.

She felt cheerful again as she walked back to the "safe" flat and packed her belongings. Then she made a quick call to her father in Putney to say she was on her way to visit them. Because of her luggage, she took a taxi, and on the way, she began thinking about the exciting new future career that had been suggested and wondered where she could find Russian lessons.

She was there in time for lunch, and to her parents' great surprise, she explained what had happened that morning and that, as a consequence, she was no longer required as a witness in a big trial of a Russian spy. Therefore, she was on her way back to Portsmouth to resume her normal life – after a far from normal few weeks.

Victor and Shona Peters were reassured by the conversation because their lives had also been disrupted for weeks with visits from the police, the security services and the man from the Russian Embassy. After a relaxed lunch, Marina kissed her mother goodbye, and Victor drove Marina to Clapham Junction to catch a train to Portsmouth.

On the way, she tried to rehearse how she would answer

calls from the press. She also made a list of all the people she now needed to contact once she had settled back into her Southsea flat: there was the helpful solicitor, Jeremy Scott, and his boss David Barclay-Smith; there was Betty, of course, and her friend Susie Mann – and Susie's parents, Admiral and Mrs. Mann; then there was her boss at the Navy Communications Office in the Dockyard to discover when to go back to work at last. So what else? There was shopping to do to restock her food store after so long away, and goodness knows what the state of her refrigerator contents might be? It was going to be back to the basics of her life again, a period of readjustment after being looked after at the MI5 flat in London and the CIA facility in Florida, not to mention the unforgettable night at the Ritz Carlton and the comfort of business class flights with BA.

At Portsmouth and Southsea station, she soon found a taxi to take her back to the familiar block of flats near the seafront. Fortunately, the press had given up watching for her return, and the final press release from the Foreign Office was about to be distributed that same evening. She found the key which opened the door to the lobby and the lift took her to the second floor and her own front door. The empty flat seemed welcoming after so long away, and she was just starting to unpack her luggage when the doorbell rang. It was, as she expected, her friendly neighbour.

"I thought we had lost you!" said Mrs. Watkins when Marina opened the door. "I just heard you arrive and it is lovely to see you again. There has been so much going on here, and we have all been very worried for you, especially after reading the papers. Are you all right?"

"Yes, thank you," said Marina. "I've had a lot going on, too, but now it is all over, and I just want to get back to normal again. I will tell you all about it one day, but right now I have to settle in, then go to the shop for some groceries while they are still open and make a few phone calls and other things. It has been weeks since I was here and I am sure I have to do some tidying up and then check the state of everything, especially the fridge."

Mrs. Watkins got the message and understood why Marina politely excused herself from an invitation to go next door for a cup of tea. "Let me know if I can help. I will see you tomorrow, if that's okay," she said as Marina closed her door.

After unpacking and hanging up her clothes, Marina turned her attention to the kitchen and soon filled a bin bag with much of the contents of her refrigerator. She worked out what she needed from the nearby one-stop shop and decided that this must be her next job. She put on her shoes again and a winter-weight coat, picked up her shopping bag and set off to walk the two blocks to buy the essentials she needed to see her through the next couple of days.

As she came back, she remembered to check her mailbox in the lobby. It was quite full, and she managed to fit a pile of correspondence, brochures and flyers into one of her shopping bags to take back to her flat. There, she put the kettle on and packed away her shopping. She made a cup of tea and started to look at her mail.

Apart from the usual junk mail, there were bills to be opened, a few personal letters and one large brown envelope which looked official – perhaps something from the Navy about my job, she thought as she pulled open the well-sealed flap ….

Immediately, a cloud of white powder flew into her face and over her neck and her bare arms. It stung, and she quickly realised that this was something serious and not some sort of practical joke. Trying to wipe her face clean and with her eyes tingling, she staggered to the phone and dialled 999.

28.
THE CRIME SCENE

Chief Constable Terence Hardy, head of the Portsmouth City Police, was at home, getting changed out of uniform and preparing for guests expected for dinner when his phone rang. It was a somewhat agitated Paul Maggs, his CID chief.

"Sorry sir, but this is important… You need to know that we have an attempted murder on our hands, and it's another stage in that Russian spy story."

This quickly alerted the chief to take the call seriously. He thought the whole thing had ended with the Foreign Officer statement about the spy exchange. He listened alertly as Maggs began to outline the events of the past two hours, which, he said, had begun with the return of Marina Peters to her flat in Southsea, also believing that the episode was now over.

"It appears that she was opening her accumulated pile of mail from several weeks away when she opened an envelope which must have contained some kind of poison," he continued. "She had the good sense to dial 999 at once, and when the paramedics arrived, they had to break into her flat and found her unconscious on the floor. They quickly recognised that she had a white powder on her face and hands, and with the Salisbury spy story still fresh in their minds, they decided not to touch her without protective clothing. They had the good sense to first call CID and then to contact the hospital for back-up by someone who understood this type of thing."

"What do they think it is?" asked the Chief Constable. "They are certainly doing the right things."

Maggs went on with his report and explained how one of the paramedics went back to their ambulance and found the protective plastic overalls, mask and gloves that they always carried, and he got close enough to ascertain that the patient was still breathing, though deeply unconscious. They made her as comfortable as possible until the emergency team arrived from the Police Station, followed by a specialist from the hospital.

"Our fellows then called me again to report the situation and said the doctor's first reaction was suspected Ricin poisoning," continued Maggs. "Well, we've all had some training on this sort of thing – and given the woman's recent history, I realised that this was probably another security situation. Then I remembered those two Russian agents we talked to a few weeks back who were apparently looking for her. If you remember, we took their pictures, and MI5 recognised them as known agents based at the Russian Embassy in London. We have their names and we know they located the woman's address.

"This is all circumstantial and guesswork at the moment, sir, but it has all the signs of an attempted murder, and I decided it was urgent enough to phone our contact at MI5. After I had briefed him, he agreed that we should take precautions to prevent any contamination from the spread of the material from the envelope and that we should get the woman to hospital quickly for a proper diagnosis – which, of course, we were already doing. He also suggested that we probably had enough information to issue an arrest warrant

The Russian Lieutenant

naming the two Russians on suspicion of attempted murder. Do you agree?"

"Absolutely," replied Terence Hardy. "Who's in charge at the scene at the moment?"

Superintendent Maggs told his chief that Detective Sergeant Bullock was there with a couple of DCs, and they were being very careful but also putting together as much evidence as they could find. It was agreed to set the wheels in motion for an arrest warrant right away and to follow up with Scotland Yard to get the Russian couple on the international wanted list at the airports and ferry ports.

Taking charge of the situation, the Chief Constable replied, "Let me know when the woman gets to hospital and also make sure we get the doctors to check out all the others who went to the scene in case they have also been infected by the Ricin, or whatever it is. And get our decontamination team on the job quickly to work on the flat and any other areas that might be affected. This is a block of flats, isn't it, so maybe they should all be evacuated while the work is being done. I think I'll call my opposite number in Salisbury to see if there is anything we haven't thought of – and I'll also let the Navy people know what's going on before they hear it from anyone else. The press are bound to be on this once we evacuate the flats, so can you get one of your people to draft a statement and let me see it before it is released."

"OK, chief. I've got all that and will stay in touch. I think I had better go to see what's happening at the flat as soon as I can."

The Chief Constable then remembered that it was his Navy friend, Commander Robert Gaffney, who was expected for dinner that evening with his wife. Simultaneously, he came to the conclusion that this was a fast-moving situation and his place was really at his office, coordinating the police operation. He made the call quickly.

"Robert, so glad I have caught you before you left home, but we have a bit of a crisis this evening. I've only just been briefed, and I was going to call you anyway. I am sure you remember the woman from your communications office who was caught up with this Russian spy business. We thought it was all done and dusted when they announced the spy swap last week, but now she has come back to her place in Southsea and has just been found unconscious – and probably poisoned."

"My God," replied Gaffney. "What's going on?"

"Well, I can't tell you much more at the moment, but I'm afraid I have to go back to the office, and we'll have to rearrange our dinner date – so sorry about that."

"Of course, I understand – but please let me know how the woman gets on. She was called Peters, so far as I can remember."

"Yes, Marina Peters – and I'll keep you in the picture, but I'll appreciate that you don't pass this on until I find out more facts."

They ended the call, and Hardy went to find his wife to tell her that the dinner party was cancelled and that he had to return to the office to deal with a crisis situation. She tried to find out more details from him, but he was now in a hurry and drove away to the Police HQ as quickly as possible.

Meanwhile, the doctor on the scene had decided that the paramedics should carefully move Marina to the Portsmouth hospital as soon as possible; he then called his specialist colleagues at the hospital about what to expect. The team carefully wrapped the patient in protective sheeting brought by the police decontamination squad and carried her out to the ambulance, watched now by the very concerned neighbours who had been evacuated from their flats. Also, there were several of the local press watching and shouting questions, and two police constables who made sure they all kept their distance. Sergeant Bullock simply confirmed to the reporters that it was, indeed, Marina Peters who was being taken to hospital and that the Chief Constable's office would provide a statement as soon as possible.

While the ambulance was on its way, the Portsmouth doctors spoke to their opposite numbers in Salisbury, and they agreed that although the Ricin powder was a poison unlike the nerve agent Novichok, there were enough similarities in the treatment regimes to compare notes regarding the approach to such a serious and potentially dangerous procedure. Once she was in the isolation section of the hospital, the trauma team, also in protective gear, began attempting to clear Marina's airways and lungs of the white poison – but her condition was deteriorating rapidly.

Meanwhile, the police officers at the Southsea flats told the anxious residents that the emergency had been created by the discovery of a dangerous substance in Miss Peters' flat on the second floor. They said there was no confirmation yet of the precise nature of the substance, but that as a precaution, it was necessary to vacate their properties while a decontamination process was carried out.

The specialists from the police emergencies unit arrived and carried out detailed checks around Marina's flat and the adjoining areas to assess the extent of the problem. The chatter among the residents and the reporters immediately made comparisons with the activity in Salisbury a few months earlier, and within an hour, the Chief Constable's office issued a brief statement to the press:

"This is to confirm that Miss Marina Peters has been discovered seriously ill at her flat in Southsea. It is Miss Peters who was involved in the recent investigations regarding a Russian agent who arrived in Portsmouth

on board the RSS Admiral Essen. She has been taken to Portsmouth hospital where she is receiving specialist attention for probable poisoning. We are currently investigating all the circumstances and have taken the precaution of evacuating the adjacent flats while tests are carried out."

Then Chief Constable Hardy had a phone call from Tom Spencer at MI5. "The birds have flown," he said. "The Border Control at Heathrow have just told us that those two Russians you saw in Portsmouth actually flew out to Moscow on the scheduled Aeroflot flight this morning. I suspect that it was the woman's phone call to her father yesterday that was picked up, and so they knew she was on her way to Portsmouth and would find the nasty surprise they had left in her flat. I think you have a case of suspected murder on your hands."

29.
WHO POISONED MARINA?

Early the next morning, the Chief Constable had a call from the hospital to confirm that yes, it was a case of Ricin poisoning and that despite their best efforts, Marina had died. Her parents had arrived at the hospital during the night but had not been able to speak to their daughter. The hospital had also carried out tests on the two ambulance crew members who had brought her in, and they were both taking antidotes and would be off duty for a few days. The police officers who went to the scene would also be checked by the hospital as soon as possible.

A very saddened Terence Hardy had quite a few calls to make to follow up this news, and he set about it right away – informing the Navy, MI5, the Coroner's office and his own officers. Then he decided he needed to call a news conference for 9 am, which was set up by his PR department.

There were half a dozen local reporters there to hear his news.

"It is with great regret that I have to tell you that Miss Marina Peters died this morning in Portsmouth hospital", he began. "She was taken there yesterday afternoon after collapsing at her flat in Southsea. I am sure I do not have to tell you about the circumstances during the recent weeks relating to Miss Peters. But I can confirm that she died as a result of Ricin poisoning, and we are treating this as a murder inquiry. We evacuated the neighbouring flats to ensure that there is no contamination as a result of the Ricin which was discovered in Miss Peters' flat. As I am sure you know, Ricin is an extremely dangerous poison. Our CID officers are carrying out investigations in conjunction with Scotland Yard and MI5, and I will give you more information in due course. Meanwhile, the Coroner has been informed, and an inquest will be opened in the next few days."

The Chief Constable took questions, but he could add very little at this stage. No, he could not yet say how the Ricin had come to be in the flat. Yes, her parents had come down from London during the night to be at her bedside. No, Miss Peters was not the subject of any further police inquiries relating to her association with the Russian spy. And finally: "Are the Russians suspected of carrying out this murder, and is there any connection between this incident and the recent Salisbury Novichok incidents?"

He replied, "It is too early to talk about suspects, but I can tell you that the doctors at Portsmouth hospital did talk to their counterparts in Salisbury last night in case there were some common elements in the treatment regime."

The next morning, the Portsmouth City Coroner, Robert Leveson QC, opened an inquest at the Guildhall and adjourned it for three weeks.

Following the brief inquest and the police statement, the Russian spy story came alive in Portsmouth again and over the following days, it was fully covered in the press and on radio and TV. Speculation inevitably pointed fingers at Russian involvement in Marina's death, but facts were hard to come by. Who had poisoned Marina, how and why? The story of Marina's interlude with the CIA in Florida was leaked in London and led to further inquiries and interviews in the States. In Moscow, reporters tried to discover more about the GRU agent who had posed as a Russian naval officer, but since the dramatic spy swap, he was being kept out of sight.

It was still a news story that had everything – a murder victim, Russian spies, the CIA – everything, that is, but facts.

It was the last week of November before the inquest into the death of Marina Peters was resumed. The first witness to appear before the Coroner was Victor Peters, who confirmed that he was the father of Marina Peters and that he had seen her frequently since she moved from London to work in Portsmouth three years ago. She had visited him and his wife in Putney on the day she died, before catching a train to Portsmouth. She had appeared to be in good health after a holiday in Canada. The Coroner thanked him and offered condolences to the family.

Next, Dr. Michael Greenslade, the senior medical officer from Portsmouth Hospital, was called, and he described how Marina had been admitted in an unconscious condition with a suspicion of Ricin poisoning.

He continued: "We immediately admitted her to our special isolated area for unusual cases and took all the necessary precautions. Although this is a very uncommon problem, our tests quickly confirmed that it was, indeed, the effects of Ricin, which is a very potent poison, and antidotes are rarely effective. We took advice from medical experts in London, but we were quite unable to reverse the deterioration in her condition, and sadly she passed away some 12 hours after her admission."

The Coroner asked Dr. Greenslade if he or his colleagues had any previous experience of Ricin poisoning.

"Fortunately, no" came the reply. "This is something which has only occurred rarely in Europe or the USA, usually connected with some sort of political assassination attempt. We have had training in all types of extreme problems, including Ricin poisoning, and there is a wealth of information available to us in the unlikely event of needing to deal with it. Bear in mind that we also had to protect our own team and to ensure that others who came into contact with the patient during the day were also tested for any possible contamination."

Mr. Leveson then asked, "Can you comment on the likely quantity of this poison which had infected the patient?"

"Not specifically, sir," replied the doctor. "There was still evidence of the white granules around her mouth and nose when she was admitted, but it takes only a very small amount of Ricin to prove fatal."

The next witness was Detective Sergeant Bullock, who described what he'd found when he and other officers arrived at the flat in response to the call from the ambulance team which had answered the original 999 call from Miss Peters.

He then continued: "They had done all they could in these circumstances and when the doctor arrived a few minutes later, he told me he suspected that it might be a case of Ricin poisoning. I recognised that this was very serious and that the flat was now a crime scene. The medical team was able to use protective coverings to get the patient down to the ambulance and then to the hospital. We also put on protective overalls and began searching for evidence, and what soon became clear was that Miss Peters had been opening a pile of incoming mail. She had been sitting on a sofa, probably with all the mail on her lap, and she had obviously been ripping the envelopes open by hand, judging from those we saw on the sofa and the floor. It appears that she tore open a large brown envelope and the contents were a quantity of white powder which spilled out. We could see that the powder had been in the air and over her face, hands and arms. There was clearly more of it in the brown envelope which lay among the other envelopes on the floor, with more signs of the powder on the carpet. We took photographs before carefully collecting as much evidence as possible for further examination. Then our decontamination team arrived from Head Office and took over control of the area.

"Next I spoke to neighbours who said that Miss Peters had been away for over three weeks, and they showed me the individually named mailboxes in the lobby where she would have found her incoming letters. The postman is usually admitted by one of the ground floor residents to deliver mail each morning, but it seems that although the main door is normally kept locked, they agreed that it is sometimes left open for deliveries and for cleaning staff, so it would not be difficult for a stranger to enter and put an envelope into a specific mailbox."

The Coroner thanked the sergeant for his full report and then called Detective Superintendent Maggs. He asked him, "What has been the result of your investigations and do you have any idea of who might be involved in this case?"

"As I am sure you know, sir, Miss Peters was involved in the situation which arose with the Russian agent who was arrested when he arrived in Portsmouth on board a Russian warship two months ago," he began. "Since then, she has been looked after by MI5 in London while they prepared their case against the detained Russian, who turned out to be an agent with the Russian Intelligence Service. She would have been a material witness in the case, but as I am sure you know, there will no longer be a court hearing because the Russian was sent back home as part of an exchange arrangement.

"During the days after our arrest of the Russian, we

became aware of a couple who were posing as relatives of Miss Peters and attempting to find her. We took surreptitious pictures of them and Scotland Yard was able to confirm that they were both known to be intelligence officers based at the Russian Embassy in London. We discovered the B&B where they had been staying for two nights and obtained some DNA evidence from their bathroom.

"There is little doubt that as members of the Russian Security Service, known as the GRU, they would have had access to substances such as Ricin. These two individuals did not find her because she had been relocated from her flat at the request of MI5, but it is a strong possibility that the Russian agents could have found a way to place the envelope in her mailbox. We put out an international search warrant for the couple, but it has now been confirmed to us that they flew back to Moscow on the same day that Miss Peters returned to Portsmouth. The whole matter is now in the hands of Scotland Yard and MI5."

"I don't suppose you had any reason to check Miss Peters' flat or her mailbox while she was away?" asked the Coroner. "And do you think the suspicious envelope was properly sealed so that it could not have been a danger to anyone else?"

"I think that is correct," said DS Maggs. "And bear in mind that Miss Peters had not committed any offence by corresponding with the Russian and had only been questioned by us and MI5 because of her importance as a potential witness."

Robert Leveson decided that he had heard enough to reach the conclusion that the death of Miss Peters had been a case of murder by person or persons unknown. He also suggested that there was another criminal offence which the police might pursue, that of causing danger to the public by carrying an illegal deadly poison and then depositing it in a public area. He was therefore in a position to authorize the issue of a death certificate to the family. However, he had decided not to close the file, pending further inquiries and the possible apprehension of the perpetrators of the crimes in due course, and he would accordingly send his report to the Chief Constable, the Home Office and all the authorities involved. He extended his sympathy to the family and to Miss Peters' friends and work colleagues in Portsmouth.

30.
A RED ROSE

Victor and Shona Peters had travelled to Portsmouth to be at the inquest, and as the witnesses and public audience slowly moved from the room, Victor was pleased to have an opportunity to chat to Betty McGuire, their daughter's best friend, whom he had met briefly on his previous trip to the city. She then introduced Marina's parents to other friends and neighbours, and soon they were also chatting in the Guildhall lobby area to some of her former Royal Navy colleagues, including the senior staff who had come from the Navy HQ. As they were all meeting each other, Victor interrupted and said, "You know, we don't know much about Marina's life here in Portsmouth – do you all have time to come over the road to the hotel for a drink or a cup of tea?"

About a dozen of the group quickly filled the hotel lounge, and orders were taken by the barman as Marina's three years in Portsmouth were relived for her parents. They were both proud and fascinated, and eventually, the subject came round to funeral arrangements. They warmed to a suggestion from Commander Gaffney that it should be a Naval occasion in Portsmouth – and Victor then explained to his rather doubtful wife: "All her friends are here, and then we can have a family memorial service in Putney later on as well."

The Commander said that as a start, he would contact the Royal Navy's senior chaplain in Portsmouth and also check the availability of the chapel in the Dockyard, St. Ann's – the "spiritual home of the Royal Navy" – with its long history. This striking red brick church was built in 1704, then badly damaged by the bombing of the Dockyard in 1943 and eventually restored in 1956. The plaques on its walls are testament to the funerals of many famous admirals over the years and the Commander said he considered that the circumstances surrounding Marina's tragic death, probably by the hands of a foreign power, fully justified this recognition.

And so the die was cast, and it was Betty and Marina's former boss, Lieutenant Anne Gleeson, head of the communications section at the Dockyard HQ, who volunteered to follow up the suggestion in more detail and make the necessary arrangements. This, said Lieut. Gleeson, would include confirming a date convenient to everyone concerned and she promised to keep Mr. and Mrs. Peters involved at all stages.

First, the two planners went together to see a local funeral director who was experienced in handling such matters for the Navy and outlined their needs. And once the date was confirmed, they began to arrange a very naval occasion at St. Ann's.

Two weeks later, the day of the funeral arrived. The solemn service was attended by more "senior brass" than they might have expected for the funeral of a relatively junior and civilian member of staff – but the story of Marina had touched many hearts.

Two young sailors in uniform acted as ushers and smartly escorted Mr. and Mrs. Peters to the front row, together with Andrew Peters and other family members who had travelled down from London for the day. They were very impressed when Commander Robert Gaffney, in full uniform, arrived in the church and strode to the front to introduce himself and to tell them that many others from the Navy headquarters team were also there to pay their respects to Marina, who had been "a wonderful colleague and a friend to them all".

Tom Spencer, his deputy Tony and Patricia from MI5 came by car from London to attend the service. They also brought with them Charles Alexander, the freed Foreign Office diplomat, who was anxious to pay his respects to the woman whose connection with the Russian agent had led to his unexpected and sudden return home. The two local solicitors, David Barclay-Smith and Jeremy Scott, sat with Chief Constable Terence Hardy, Detective Superintendent Maggs and others from the local police station. Matthew Sampson, editor of the Weekly Herald, was at the back, together with his reporters, Gary Andrews and Charles Williams, plus Mike Morrissey the freelance. (Not surprisingly, all three were also interested in writing the next news story about Marina's funeral and also the possible opportunity it provided to talk afterwards to some of those involved in the investigation!)

Betty arrived with Susie and her parents, Rear Admiral and Mrs. Mann. Also there were Mrs. Watkins, the helpful neighbour, who came with at least six more residents from the Southsea flats. There were many others among the mourners who felt they "knew" Marina from all the publicity in the press and on TV.

It was therefore a very mixed – and distinguished – group who filled the seats in the small church as the organist played music from "Portsmouth Point", an overture written by the English composer William Walton and inspired by life at the seaport. Then the chaplain led a very naval service with appropriate hymns, including "For Those in Peril on the Sea". In his address, he lamented Marina's sad passing and talked about the important job she had been doing for the Navy and for her nation's defence. He emphasized how much she was missed by everyone in the department where she worked – and how much they also missed her optimistic view of life, which had influenced them all. Marina's uncle Andrew, in his clear though slightly accented English, gave the eulogy on behalf of the family, in which he told the story of her early life, her successes at school and university and her quiet ambition and determination to succeed in whatever she chose to do.

Noticeably, to some of those present, nowhere in the service was there any reference to Russia – neither the family's ancestry nor Marina's more recent involvement.

As the service ended, the congregation began to move out with the organist playing the rousing melody of "Hearts of Oak", and there was an invitation on the Order of Service cards for everyone to gather again at 2 pm in Old Portsmouth and to join the family for refreshments – and more reminiscences – at the Sally Port Hotel.

Meanwhile, the coffin, borne by six uniformed sailors, was carried to the hearse at the door, followed by Marina's parents and her uncle Andrew. Another vehicle was also there to take them, following the hearse, for a small, private farewell at the Portsmouth Crematorium. Afterwards, the family was driven back to Old Portsmouth and to the gathering of so many who had been involved in their daughter's life in the Navy and her final tragic weeks. The conversations and refreshments were well under way when they arrived, and Victor sought out Commander Gaffney to thank him for the generosity of whoever had organised such a special occasion and offering to pay whatever it had cost. "We will always remember Marina and this day," he said.

And the Commander replied, "It's the Navy's way of

recognising the service of a shipmate who has been lost to us in such tragic circumstances. You all have our deepest condolences, and you can be sure that your daughter will be long remembered by us, too."

A little later, the funeral director arrived carrying a discrete brass urn containing Marina's ashes. The chaplain called for attention and invited everyone to follow him and the funeral director; a group of about 60 or 70 then walked the 400 yards to the sea wall by the old Semaphore Tower.

As they walked, Victor realised that he had not previously spotted the presence of his contact, "Jack", from the Russian Embassy in London. He briefly slipped away from Shona's side and moved to join the Russian to make a point of telling him firmly: "You are not welcome here, and I want nothing more to do with my daughter's killers, ever."

"Jack" then drifted to the back of the crowd ... but still followed.

It was one of those cold but clear late November afternoons without a breath of wind, and as the large group crowded together on the sea wall, with the background of waves lapping gently against the stones, the chaplain moved to the front and began by recalling: "This is where the last, sad chapter in Marina's life actually began, just 10 weeks ago. As she told her close friends, this is where she planned to stand to watch the arrival of the ship which she hoped would bring something new and important into her life. Yes, many of us think about new beginnings at some time, and this was what Marina was seeking. Instead, we now gather here to mourn her sudden departure to a rather different new beginning, in the care of our Lord. And now, in a traditional naval way, Victor and Shona will scatter her ashes into the sea which had become the new focus in those last three years of her short life."

Marina's parents stepped forward to take the urn from

the funeral director, and up above them on the Semaphore tower was a Royal Marine bugler who sounded the Last Post, its melancholic final notes echoing across the ancient stone walls. There were tears among many of those watching as the ashes fluttered down into the waters of Spithead.

And then, without a word, "Jack" suddenly stepped forward from the group and silently cast a single red rose into the water. He handed the chaplain a card to be read to the mourners:

"Farewell Marina. I am so sorry – it was not supposed to end like this. Rest in Peace – from your Russian Lieutenant."

Lightning Source UK Ltd.
Milton Keynes UK
UKHW041147131120
373341UK00004B/567